It was Amy who spoke first. "Marketa and I had a crazy idea."

Ondrej settled into one of the cushy chairs and waited.

Marketa said, "I understand you wish to stay in this country."

Ondrej looked around. "Are you offering me a job?" "No," said Archie. "Unfortunately, I can't afford to hire you full-time. This would be a different sort of arrangement."

Ondrej glanced at the unknown man in the room. He wanted to inquire who the man was, but he was too confused to speak.

Marketa said, "I'll be frank. We run background checks on all new hires, and something interesting came up in yours."

Ondrej knew in a flash that they'd cottoned on to his net worth. "My money," he said.

The unknown man leaned forward. "Mr. Katsaros wishes to make a proposal."

Welcome to

⊚REAMSPUN DESIRES

Dear Reader,

Love is the dream. It dazzles us, makes us stronger, and brings us to our knees. Dreamspun Desires tell stories of love featuring your favorite heartwarming heroes, captivating plots, and exotic locations. Stories that make your breath catch and your imagination soar.

In the pages of these wonderful love stories, readers can escape to a world where love conquers all, the tenderness of a first kiss sweeps you away, and your heart pounds at the sight of the one you love.

When you put it all together, you find romance in its truest form.

Love always finds a way.

Elizabeth North

Executive Director
Dreamspinner Press

Kate McMurray

THE GREEK TYCOON'S GREEN CARD GROOM

ᎠREAMSPUN DESIRES

PUBLISHED BY

ᎠREAMSPINNER
PRESS

Published by
DREAMSPINNER PRESS

5032 Capital Circle SW, Suite 2, PMB# 279,
Tallahassee, FL 32305-7886 USA
www.dreamspinnerpress.com

The Greek Tycoon's Green Card Groom
© 2016 Kate McMurray.

Cover Art
© 2016 Bree Archer.
http://www.breearcher.com
Cover content is for illustrative purposes only and any person depicted
on the cover is a model.

ISBN: 978-1-63477-086-6
Digital ISBN: 978-1-63477-087-3
Library of Congress Control Number: 2016907747
Published July 2016
v. 1.0

Printed in the United States of America
∞
This paper meets the requirements of
ANSI/NISO Z39.48-1992 (Permanence of Paper).

KATE MCMURRAY is an award-winning romance author and fan. When she's not writing, she works as a nonfiction editor, dabbles in various crafts, and is maybe a tiny bit obsessed with baseball. She is active in RWA and has served as president of Rainbow Romance Writers and on the board of RWANYC. She lives in Brooklyn, NY.

Website: www.katemcmurray.com

Twitter: www.twitter.com/katemcmwriter

Facebook: www.facebook.com/katemcmurraywriter

Acknowledgments

THANK you to Poppy Dennison for talking me into this and being as delighted as I was to revisit my old collection of category romances from the eighties, which served as inspiration for this novel. Thanks, too, to the Brooklyn Public Library for having so many Harlequin Presents in its collection. And a special thank you to Damon Suede, who helped with the title before this book even had a plot.

Chapter One

"**SIGN** here."

Ondrej nearly balked, wondering if he wasn't signing his soul over to the devil. Certainly Archimedes Katsaros was the very picture of the devil, especially in the way his eyebrows now came to an angry point just above his nose. His neatly trimmed goatee wrapped around his chin, and his dark, curly hair hung near his eyes. A handsome devil, sure, but a devil just the same.

Still, Ondrej picked up the pen and glanced at the document on the counter before glancing back up at the clerk.

Archie Katsaros glared. "What is the hesitation, my love?"

"This is a significant moment, darling. I was merely pausing to soak it all in." Ondrej took a deep breath and signed on the line.

The clerk beamed at them. "Congratulations, you two! I now pronounce you husband and husband." She giggled. "Oh, I love doing that! Kiss!"

Archie raised an eyebrow and leaned forward, so Ondrej gave him a quick peck for appearances.

"That was so tame." The clerk clucked her tongue. "Well, I can't say this office is the most romantic place ever. I'll bet you'll wait to do more until you're behind closed doors later, huh?" She gathered up the papers Ondrej and Archie had just signed. "I'll be right back. Bask in the moment!"

"Some moment," Ondrej muttered.

"It could be much worse."

Ondrej looked over Archie again. He agreed that there were a lot of ways this situation could be worse. Archie could be a woman, for one thing. At least this way, Ondrej wouldn't have to fake attraction, even if he didn't think much of his new husband as a person.

And to think, three months ago, before Ondrej's work visa expired, he'd been a mere intern at Katsaros Holdings, a large New York real estate firm. Ondrej had just wanted something to do for a summer that involved not getting yelled at by his mother. He was lazy, she said, and how could such a sweet boy not want to marry the Reznik girl, whose family was as wealthy as Ondrej's? So Ondrej had fled to the US, thinking he could kill a summer with odd jobs and men without the specter of his family hovering over him. He had a strong enough business background that the people he interviewed with at Katsaros had practically fallen over themselves to offer him a low-paying position. So he had agreed to the short-term internship and planned to spend the summer learning about American business and living it up in the city before returning to Prague.

Except when the internship ended and Ondrej was out of a job, he realized he loved New York. It felt like home in a way Prague never had. He wanted to stay.

Enter Archimedes Katsaros.

The whole agreeing-to-get-married thing wasn't a completely desperate act, but Ondrej had begun to panic after a few weeks of unemployment. With summer over, no one was hiring, or else he was competing with college kids for whom employers had to do less paperwork for the few open jobs. When he got a call from the USCIS saying if he didn't find a job within a set amount of time, he'd have to go back to Prague, Ondrej freaked out. He had consulted the only person he could think of to help him: his former boss at Katsaros Holdings. She'd nudged him toward this somewhat unorthodox solution.

It had seemed crazy at first. Ondrej had refused the first time Archie suggested this scheme. But the more he looked at Archie Katsaros—the more his lust for the handsome devil grew—the less insane the idea seemed.

It wasn't a one-sided agreement. Ondrej had inherited a pile of money from his grandparents, who'd owned a winery in France. Archie needed a windfall to prop up a company that had been flailing since the death of his father, as he was now teetering on the edge of bankruptcy, despite the company's public reputation for being a solid corporation. So in exchange for marrying Archie in order to stay in the States, Ondrej promised to invest some of his money in Katsaros Holdings. And wouldn't sharing his inheritance with a male spouse really get his mother's goat?

Archie did have three things going for him: he was a US citizen, he was gay, and he was dead sexy. This whole proposition was the most reckless thing Ondrej had ever done, and yet it still didn't feel like the worst idea ever.

So now here they were. Married.

The clerk returned, a wide grin on her face. "All right, Mr. Katsaros and Mr…. Kovac." She pronounced it Ko-vack. "Um. How do you say your first name, sir?"

"Like Andre. On-dray Ko-vatch."

"Sure. Well. Congrats again, gentlemen. Any honeymoon plans?"

"Actually, we—" Ondrej started to say.

But Archie talked over him. "I plan to whisk my new husband away to the Florida Keys. He hasn't seen much of this country outside of New York City, and I want to show him what else is here."

"Oh, that will be delightful. My sister went to Key Largo on her honeymoon."

The legal bit taken care of, Ondrej figured now he only had to worry about how to break the news that he'd eloped with his former boss to his friends and family.

As they walked out of the courthouse, Ondrej asked, "We aren't actually going to Florida, are we?"

"We can if you like. I reasoned that with your fragile immigration status, we'd probably have to stay in the States until the paperwork is done. It is customary to go on some kind of honeymoon, right?"

Ondrej sighed. The prospect of spending a week or two cooped up with a man he barely knew was daunting. "It's… we don't have to go anywhere. This isn't a real marriage. And you just told me last week you don't have time for a vacation."

Archie frowned. "That is true." He glanced at his watch. "In fact, I should probably get back to the office right now." They arrived at the corner, and Archie moved as though he were about to hail a cab.

"Such a romantic," Ondrej said. "Spending your wedding day at the office."

"You can't have it both ways, sweetheart," Archie said, raising his hand to hail a cab. "We either acknowledge this fraud and go back to what we were doing yesterday or we try to make the most of it. Personally, I've got a meeting with an architect about a new development tomorrow, and I still have a lot of prep work."

So clearly Archie had made a decision that this was a business transaction and nothing more. Ondrej could work with that. "I was kidding."

"Sure." A cab pulled up. "You coming back to the office?"

"I'll get the subway home," Ondrej said. "Might as well finish unpacking."

ARCHIE was related on his mother's side to some old New York money, and the house just off Fifth Avenue on the Upper East Side had been passed down through a few generations. For a house in a city that put a premium on space, it was too much: sprawling and conspicuously opulent, full of antiques and marble and chandeliers—a palace, essentially, though a lot of it was also dusty, worn, and threadbare, a remnant of a past era. Ondrej supposed that when one was trying to bail out an international corporation, one didn't have many resources left to put toward upkeep at home, save for Hildy the maid, who only came by once a week.

She was there sweeping the front foyer when Ondrej walked in after the wedding. "Hello, Mr. Kovac. Welcome home."

Ondrej thanked her and walked to the grand staircase. After months of hopping around between hotels and temporary sublets, it was strange to have a place to call home. And there were certainly worse homes than a 140-year-old mansion in New York City.

As he walked to his bedroom, he mused that at least only having Hildy instead of a whole passel of servants made this particular little ruse easier. Or big ruse. Archie was broke, but very few people knew that. Archie and Ondrej had been purposefully going out together in order to be seen, to play up their whirlwind romance for the society pages, even though they barely liked each other and had separate bedrooms at home. The public appearances were at Archie's insistence; they weren't important or interesting enough to snare much media attention, but Archie kept talking about appearances. It would seem convenient if they'd never been seen out together before they got married. Living in the same house lent the marriage some legitimacy. But living in the same bedroom felt like too much.

Ondrej went to his room and surveyed the great pile of luggage at the foot of the bed. It had been delivered that very morning from the hotel where Ondrej had been crashing for the past week. He'd accumulated a surprising amount of stuff in his short few months in New York. He was reluctant to take most of it out of the suitcases, still convinced he'd have to live out of them for a while longer, not believing that this was really his house. But legally it was; the marriage license tucked into his jacket pocket said as much.

But a marriage to Archimedes Katsaros was not at all what he'd pictured when he imagined his life in America.

Ondrej's bedroom had a walk-in closet, because of course it did. Whoever had built this house had spared no expense. As he put his clothes away, Ondrej tried to reconcile this giant house with what he'd seen so far in New York. He'd stayed in hotel rooms smaller than the closet, places that had insects and lumpy mattresses despite costing more than a week's pay per night. But this room was well-appointed, if plain. Someone—and given how old everything was, someone back a few generations—had spent a great deal of money outfitting this house. How had Katsaros Holdings squandered the Katsaros fortune and Archie's mother's fortune as well? It must have been a considerable fortune if this was the family home. Was Ondrej's money just going to disappear into the same black hole?

"I'm going, Mr. Kovac!" Hildy called from downstairs. "Have a great day!"

The front door closed with a thud. Ondrej was alone in the house. In *his* house, he reminded himself. Which meant that even though he still felt like a guest, he could—and should—go exploring.

Curiosity led him straight to Archie's room. Ondrej had seen it in passing when he'd moved in, and he'd had all sorts of expectations for what the bedroom of a failed tyrant must look like—a lot of red, was what Ondrej had been expecting—but actually, the room was mostly beige with dark blue accents, tastefully decorated, and dominated by a huge four-poster bed. The bed was neatly made, but then, Hildy had just been here. There was a huge mahogany dresser as well as a walk-in closet that Ondrej was delighted to learn was chaotic instead of neatly organized.

Ondrej searched the room, looking for some clue about who the hell Archimedes Katsaros really was, but he didn't find much. A couple of photos sat on the dresser—Ondrej's new in-laws, presumably—and a beat-up paperback novel lay on the nightstand, but otherwise nothing here said much about Archie's personality.

As Ondrej yawned, he concluded that most of the good stuff was probably in the home office, whichever room that was. Archie had given him the briefest of tours when he'd arrived that morning, but four or five rooms had closed doors. If Ondrej lived here now, wasn't it his right to get into those rooms? If he was giving Archie his money, didn't he have a right to know where it was going?

Man, that bed looked inviting.

The bed in Ondrej's room had been made too, but it wasn't nearly so nice. The ugly bedspread had probably been in the house since it was built. Maybe after the house tour, Ondrej would run out and buy some new bedding. But maybe first he'd lie down on Archie's bed. Just to test it out and see if it was as comfortable as it looked. He'd just lie down and close his eyes and....

"What the hell are you doing in here?"

Ondrej awoke with a start. The first thing he saw when he opened his eyes was Archie towering over him.

"Sorry. Guess I fell asleep."

Archie let out an exasperated sigh. "Last I checked, your bed was in the bedroom down the hall. The separate bedroom was at your insistence, was it not?"

"Yes, but—"

"I mean, if we're going to have this big, messy fraud of a marriage, might as well keep things completely separate, except when we have to go outside and pretend we're passionately in love."

"Archie, I'm sorry, but—"

"This whole thing is so fucking ridiculous, I can't...." Archie threw his hands in the air and stalked away. "What are you even doing in here, anyway?"

Ondrej couldn't say much to defuse the situation. "Look, I was just poking around this floor after I unpacked, and I saw your bed, and I wanted to see how comfortable it was. I fell asleep. So apparently it's really comfortable."

Archie took a deep breath and dropped his arms. "That's all?"

"Yeah, that's all. Why? You hiding something in here?"

"No, but... it's still weird having you in my space."

Ondrej sat up slowly. "Better get used to it. We are legally married, and you invited me to live here."

Archie frowned. "It's not that I don't want you in the house."

"You just don't want me in your personal space. I get it."

Ondrej stood and gave the room one last once-over. It really was a nice bedroom. Ondrej wondered if a possibility existed of a future in which he shared this bedroom with Archie. Of course, the man was stewing now, his arms crossed over his chest as he scowled at Ondrej, but Ondrej didn't think it was a completely repellant possibility. Maybe eventually they could become friends, or even lovers.

However, for now, Ondrej needed to get away from that furrowed brow. "I'll just go finish unpacking, yes?"

"Ondrej... I didn't mean to yell."

"It's all right."

"We're strangers, though. I understand that we're married, but we barely know each other, and I—"

"Archie, it's fine. I understand completely. Uh, will there be dinner or something?"

"Yeah, I... I ordered food from this place on Amsterdam. I just need to heat it up in the oven. Italian, if that's okay."

"That sounds great."

Archie nodded and then stalked toward the door. "Great. Kitchen table in half an hour." And with that, he stormed out of the room.

Chapter Two

ARCHIE felt strange about being in his house after a major life change with so much seeming the same. Ondrej rattling around in the house was new, and that was even stranger as Archie focused on every creak of footsteps on the old floors, every whoosh of water through the pipes, every sound that rang as a reminder there was someone else in the house.

But Ondrej had made it clear there would be no honeymoon, so Archie had sought the refuge of his office, where he sat now, staring unseeing at his laptop screen. He'd come here on the pretense of getting more work done, as if he'd been able to concentrate on anything but Ondrej all afternoon.

Ondrej was a conundrum. Somehow it had only been a couple of months since Archie had walked down to ask something of one of his executives and spotted a handsome man on the other side of the conference room.

It was like lightning had struck. Archie had to know who this man was.

The man had dark hair that hung in his eyes, and he wore an outfit that was really too casual for the office—jeans and a collared shirt with colorful stripes. Archie was struck dumb for a moment as he gazed across the sea of desks and cubicles, as the most beautiful man he'd ever seen smiled at one of the women who worked in accounts payable.

"Sir?" asked Amy, one of the managers Archie had just been talking with.

"Apologies, but who *is* that? The underdressed man talking to Frieda?"

Amy looked across the way. She nodded when she saw to whom Archie was referring. "Ah. That's Ondrej. My new intern."

"He's a little old to be an intern, isn't he?"

"He's not American, and he's only here for the summer. He's kind of an ideal intern, actually, because he's not angling for a permanent job. He came with quite a bit of business experience working for his family in Eastern Europe, and he wasn't put off by the pittance salary I offered."

Archie couldn't take his eyes off the man. He must have noticed, because this Ondrej lifted his head and met Archie's gaze. It was intense, so Archie looked away. "Wow," he whispered.

Amy chuckled. "And he's smoking hot, right?"

Archie felt the blush come to his face, but he covered it by coughing and turning his attention back to the meeting. To cover his embarrassment, he snapped at one of the people gathered. It did not befit the CEO of a major real estate firm to be blushing in response to the relative attractiveness of his employees. He felt like kind of a letch for being so struck by this man, even.

But for the rest of the day, he hadn't been able to get Ondrej out of his head. The very next day, he'd decided to go see Amy on flimsy pretenses so that he could be near Ondrej again. He'd gotten more attractive overnight, if that was possible. Archie had to be near him, had to know more about him. So he struck up a conversation while he waited for Amy to come back from a meeting.

"How are you liking the work here so far?" Archie asked.

"I like it," Ondrej said, though he hesitated before he spoke.

Was he feeling intimidated by Archie, given Archie's role in the company? "You can speak freely."

"Well, sir, I like working for Amy a great deal. But it's strange to take an internship after all the work I did back home."

"Amy said you worked for your family."

Ondrej shrugged. "Among other things."

Archie liked Ondrej's accent. It wasn't very prominent, but it definitely wasn't American. That somehow made Ondrej even sexier.

Hoping not to come across as the creepy boss preying on an underling, he started quizzing Ondrej on a few basic business principles. Ondrej answered all of the questions well, and by the time Amy returned, Ondrej had impressed the hell out of Archie in almost every way possible.

And now they were married.

AFTER dinner, Ondrej retreated to the sofa in the den, wondering if living with Archie would always feel this tense.

Perhaps marrying Archie was reckless, but there was a certain logic to it too. He'd mentioned to his boss, Amy, that his work visa was about to end but that he wanted to stay in the States and was having trouble finding another job. He'd mentioned also that the visa thing was especially frustrating because he could afford to support himself in New York indefinitely. "Wait," she'd said, "you can pay your own way? In New York City? Have you noticed how expensive it is?"

He'd shrugged. "I inherited some money from my grandparents."

But Amy must have been onto him, because she'd joked, "Well, in that case, maybe you should just get a green card marriage."

And it *had* been a joke, at first. But she must have mentioned it to Archie's secretary, Marketa, who called him into a meeting with Archie at the end of his internship.

Ondrej walked into that conference room assuming he was going to do some kind of exit interview in which he'd talk about his experience working for Katsaros Holdings. He was instead met with Archie, Marketa, Amy, and a man he didn't recognize.

It was Amy who spoke first. "Marketa and I had a crazy idea."

Ondrej settled into one of the cushy chairs and waited.

Marketa said, "I understand you wish to stay in this country."

Ondrej looked around. "Are you offering me a job?"

"No," said Archie. "Unfortunately, I can't afford to hire you full-time. This would be a different sort of arrangement."

Ondrej glanced at the unknown man in the room. He wanted to inquire who the man was, but he was too confused to speak.

Marketa said, "I'll be frank. We run background checks on all new hires, and something interesting came up in yours."

Ondrej knew in a flash that they'd cottoned on to his net worth. "My money," he said.

The unknown man leaned forward. "Mr. Katsaros wishes to make a proposal."

"Who are you?" Ondrej asked. "I know everyone else in the room, but I don't know you, sir."

"This is my attorney," said Archie. "He's drafted up an agreement that I'd like you to look at. No pressure to say yes, but I think I've found a solution to both of our problems."

Baffled, Ondrej stared at Archie. "You want me to help you with a problem?"

"How much are you willing to pay to stay in the United States?" asked Marketa.

Ondrej looked down at the contract the attorney had handed him. He scanned the first few pages and quickly determined what Archie was proposing. A green card marriage, in exchange for a good deal of money.

"This is insane," Ondrej said.

"I know. I agree." Archie stood. "Marketa came to me with this idea, and I said the same thing. But it is kind of logical." He started to pace and cleared his throat. "You're a smart man. You've probably gleaned that the financial forecast for Katsaros Holdings is not good. An influx of cash would help keep us afloat long enough for us to reorganize and restrategize. And I really hate to make something like this into such a cold, businesslike proposal, but we don't know each other very well, so I don't know how else to do this."

Ondrej understood now. He stared at the document.

"You want a way to stay in this country," said the attorney. "Mr. Katsaros is giving you one."

This was true. And still Ondrej said, "You all don't think it's strange for two men to be marrying each other? For a green card?"

"I'm gay," Archie said. "Maybe Amy was mistaken, but she said you were too. This way, at least the relationship is plausible."

"I... yes." It was hard to argue that point.

"So we have a city hall wedding," Archie went on. "Not the most romantic, perhaps. Then we'd have to make a few public appearances, make it seem convincing. We'll have to tangle with immigration, probably." He walked back to his chair and put his hands on the back of it, leaning forward slightly. "I know it sounds nuts, but I think it could work. Obviously, you can say no, but... what do you think?"

And because Ondrej was caught up in the moment and couldn't see a better solution, he said, "I... I'll do it."

It was now a few weeks later, and Ondrej was legally married to Archie Katsaros and living in his house, which should have been momentous, a joyful occasion, perhaps, but it felt more surreal than anything else.

Chapter Three

AFTER lunch with his old boss, Amy, Ondrej thought he'd drop by the office to see Archie. When he arrived at the executive suite, he could hear Archie's voice rumbling through the reception area. "Bad day?" he asked Marketa.

"The Greek economy," said Marketa. "It's been an ongoing problem. I don't know the particulars, but as of today, some of the Katsaros money is frozen, at least in the short term. He's been on the phone all morning trying to transfer his funds before they evaporate."

Marketa's tone was cheery, but her stern facial expression said she knew how dire the situation was. Archie bellowed something incoherent from inside the office.

"He still has money tied up in the Greek banks?" Ondrej suspected once again that by committing even a fraction of his fortune to Katsaros Holdings, he was kissing it good-bye.

"The late Mr. Katsaros insisted," said Marketa. "Something about preserving the Katsaros cultural legacy. Our Mr. Katsaros has been reluctant to go against anything his father established, and so here we are."

Something crashed in the office, and Archie cursed loudly and colorfully.

Ondrej looked at Marketa with alarm. She merely glanced at her phone. "He's off the line now, if you'd like to go see him."

"Maybe announce I'm here first. He'll bite my head off otherwise."

"Like a praying mantis," she said, picking up the phone.

"A praying mantis?"

"They mate and then the female bites the head off the male." She dialed. "Hello, Mr. Katsaros. Your husband is here." She listened for a moment. "Of course, sir. Right away." Then she hung up. "You may go in to see him now."

Ondrej went to Archie's door with a great deal of reluctance. What he found there surprised him, however.

Archie sat at his desk, head in his hands. "Close the door," he said as Ondrej walked in.

"Hi. I just stopped by to have lunch with Amy, so I figured I'd say hello to you too, husband of mine."

Archie looked up and nodded slowly. "Hello. It's nice to see you."

Archie delivered the words in so flat a tone, Ondrej didn't believe them. So he cut to the bigger issue. "That was quite a display."

Archie frowned. "You heard that?"

"Parts of the Bronx heard that."

"I don't normally lose my temper to that degree." Archie rubbed his face. "I'm facing something of a crisis, though, I'll have you know."

"Yes, Marketa mentioned. You have money in Greek banks?"

Archie groaned. "Do you have any notion of how difficult it is to honor the memory of a man who thought loyalty to his home country and his family was more important than practicality? That the utter failure of the Greek economy means a good chunk of his money is basically gone? All I want is to get most of what's left moved to a more stable bank." Archie sighed. "I have other money, but just… this is what I'm dealing with today. And dealing with this week. This month. This whole fucking year."

Ondrej felt like he'd been shown a glimpse under the curtain but not the whole scene. He helped himself to one of the spare office chairs. "So talk to me about the situation."

Archie tilted his head and furrowed his brow. "You're asking me about the financial situation at the company?"

Ondrej had never really asked before, but he wanted to know where his money was going. He knew Katsaros Holdings was in trouble, enough that Ondrej's money enticed Archie, but he had no idea how far in the hole the company was. Quite a bit, if Archie's distress was anything to go by. "I'm investing in your company," Ondrej reminded him.

Archie appeared to hesitate, holding up his hand and leaning back a little. But then he nodded. "I suppose it is your right to know."

ONDREJ was close, and he smelled good. Ondrej's dark hair shone in the harsh fluorescent office lighting, his skin looked soft, and his aftershave or cologne or whatever was doing some wicked things to Archie's body. Although Archie understood the importance of the numbers in the spreadsheet before him, he would rather have been talking about just about anything else.

But he explained the figures on the screen, and the bottom line was that the great Alexander Katsaros had been a keen businessman through the seventies and eighties, but he had never quite adapted to modernity, so when the rest of the world changed the way it did business in the nineties, Katsaros Holdings was left behind. Of course, no one knew that, because Alexander Katsaros was much better at maintaining his image than he was at finance. He'd taken Archie under his wing, grooming him to take over the company, and he continued to spend his wife's money to keep the company afloat long after she'd succumbed to cancer. Archie'd had no idea the company was so far in the hole until Alexander Katsaros left this mortal coil eight months ago, and thinking about the mess he'd inherited still overwhelmed him.

Worse, the executive board was starting to make noise about selling the company or wresting the management reins from Archie—something Archie could not allow. He often heard the words "hostile takeover" in his nightmares.

He didn't want to reveal the depths of his father's mismanagement just yet, but he showed Ondrej the real truth, which was that the company was in the red with no clear way out, or at least not one Archie liked.

He could sell assets, which the board was urging, or lay off employees, but he wasn't prepared to do any of that yet, not until he exhausted all other options. Unfortunately, the current state of Katsaros Holdings was like a gunshot victim who had just arrived in the ER. It was apparent the situation was dire, but Archie didn't have a firm grasp on where all the wounds were. The situation terrified Archie, and he knew he wasn't managing his stress very well, but it was all he could do to hold himself together.

But then there was Ondrej. The wedding had been one more thing on Archie's schedule the previous week, or that was how he'd tried to treat it. He hadn't been entirely successful. It felt… momentous, even if it hadn't been much more than a transaction. But Ondrej sat beside him now and looked at his computer screen, and he was just… he was right there. Archie didn't want to let himself get distracted, but it was difficult.

The thing was, Ondrej was beautiful. Archie had thought so from the first moment he'd spotted him across the office. He had dark hair and pouty lips and habitually wore a facial expression that showed he thought he was above office drudgery. Probably he really wasn't—and the expression was likely bred into him by his aristocratic upbringing and European prep school education—but Archie wanted to put him on a pedestal and admire him anyway.

It still boggled Archie's mind that Ondrej had been relegated to the role of an intern. He was clearly a whiz with numbers and had a good head for finance, which had been evident in the reports he'd prepared that had made their way to Archie's desk. Ondrej's logic and savvy with numbers had caught Archie's eye even before he'd made the connection that the person who wrote these and Amy's beautiful intern were the same person.

Of course, Ondrej had a stubborn streak and could be something of a snob, but Archie almost liked that about him, thought them kindred spirits. Part of him even wanted Ondrej to persist in his delusions that everything would always be all right, because it would spare him the pain of the rude awakening Archie'd received upon his father's death.

Ondrej looked over the numbers in Archie's spreadsheets, occasionally pointing out errors and commenting on how Archie could move funds around to make things run more efficiently.

"You're good at this," Archie said.

Ondrej waved his hand dismissively. "I've studied business. And it's my money at stake. Although I wish you'd told me how far over your head the water had risen before I consented to all this."

"I didn't know the scope of it until recently."

"How could you not know? Were you not in charge of the company?"

"No. My father was. Unfortunately he kept a lot from me." Archie took a deep breath. "My goal is to dig us out without many people knowing how bad things are. I want to protect his legacy. And I'd like to do it without laying off half my staff."

"That may not be possible."

"I realize that." Archie looked Ondrej over again. "This is quite the arrangement we have. I'm letting you into the inner circle. I don't do that with many people."

"I imagine there are many people who keep big secrets from their spouses. You and I still barely know each other."

Archie pressed his lips together and looked at his monitor. This was how the argument had been going all week. Anytime he suggested they make a go of some kind of relationship or try to learn about one another—which was what he'd wanted before they'd cooked up this harebrained marriage scheme—Ondrej pointed out that they barely knew each other.

But Archie did know Ondrej. Maybe not the way spouses who'd known each other for years did, but he knew what Ondrej was made of, where he came from, a little of the way his mind worked. Like Archie, Ondrej had grown up in the lap of luxury that somehow still left him unsatisfied. On top of that, Ondrej could be grouchy, could be cocky, could be stubborn—among his less desirable qualities—but he could also be funny, he had one of the sharpest minds Archie had ever seen, and he was always kind to new people he met.

Currently he was turning his analytic mind toward the problem of Katsaros Holdings and how it would make payroll in a few months, and he knew better than to say something like "Well, you need to bring in more income," which was what Archie's accountant had told him three weeks ago. To which Archie had responded, "Right, why didn't I think of that?" as deadpan as he could. But Ondrej said, "All right, if you take some of the money from the property on Broadway for payroll, we can put some of the Kovac money into the new development, which I feel better about." He picked up a pencil and pointed the eraser side toward the screen, showing Archie how he could move his money around to pay everyone who needed to be paid. "But I think it would be prudent to lay off a few people. Talk to your middle managers and start looking for dead weight."

It galled Archie to think of his employees in that way, but he nodded slowly, knowing that if he could streamline the sales and marketing departments, they'd still be as productive but he wouldn't have to pay as many salaries. He knew full well he was paying a few of those sales managers to surf the Internet all day. "I'll schedule a meeting."

"Good." Ondrej pushed his chair away from the desk a little. "I didn't mean to come in here and tell you how to run your business."

"You did. But it's fine. You're right, it's your money."

Ondrej pursed his lips. "Well, I guess I'll go… home."

Archie wondered if Ondrej's frown was for the prospect of a home that was still so strange or the prospect of all the idle hours before him. Had Archie been in his shoes, the latter would have filled him with dread. "You know, there's an empty office down the hall." It had been Archie's before his father died; it seemed logical for the CEO of Katsaros Holdings to occupy the CEO's office, so Archie had moved without finding another resident for his old space.

"Are you offering me a job?" Ondrej asked.

Archie thought quickly and realized he had a good option that would work for them both. "I'm offering you a partnership. You invested money in the company. I know you want some control over how it's spent. I'll put you on the board and give you a say in some day-to-day operations. In exchange, we can work out some kind of profit-sharing arrangement."

Ondrej tilted his head. "Are you willing to put this in writing?"

"Of course. Although, need I remind you, we're married."

"A joint bank account?"

"Perhaps. Kind of a unique spin on a profit-sharing plan."

As Ondrej appeared to think it over, Archie spent a moment reeling from all he'd just said. He'd married Ondrej Kovac, the most beautiful, brilliant man he'd ever known, and it would have been a dream if Ondrej weren't so determined to keep Archie at arm's length. They'd been married for almost a week and they still hadn't so much as kissed; at the house, they were ships passing in the night.

"Marriage is a long-term proposition," Archie said.

Ondrej looked up. His eyes were wide. "I suppose, yes. I mean, it could be a while until I get my green card. A year, probably."

"Perhaps instead of you continuing to tell me we hardly know each other, we could try to rectify that." Archie considered how to phrase what he wanted in a way Ondrej would respond to. "If nothing else, if we have some rapport, it would go a long way toward convincing immigration we're madly in love."

Ondrej nodded, but his face was blank, betraying no emotion. "That is true."

"More to the point, things with us would be less awkward."

Ondrej kept nodding.

Archie sighed. "That is, if I wanted an emotionless sham of a marriage, I could have married a woman. It might have been easier."

Ondrej scoffed. "Easier for whom?"

"My family. The public. Me, even. Ever since the wedding announcement hit the *Times*, my phone has been ringing off the hook from magazines and websites that want interviews with the openly gay CEO newlywed. You know they're calling me the gay Aristotle Onassis?"

"Does that make me Jackie?" Ondrej asked.

Archie laughed at how absurd it all was. "Better dust off your Chanel suits." He shook his head. "Lord, somewhere my father is turning over in his grave."

"Did he know?"

"That I'm gay? Probably. I never told him, though. Not explicitly, anyway. I mostly snuck around with my dates. Dad and I had a strict Don't Ask, Don't Tell policy in place." Archie stood up and stretched his arms. "Anyway, you could have married a woman too, but would you have wanted to?"

"No. You're right. I don't think I could pull that off."

"So we might as well make the most of the situation. I'm happy to have some help with the financial decisions, if nothing else."

Ondrej stood. "You really are in over your head."

"I believe the situation is salvageable, but it will be a challenge." An understatement, Archie knew, but he didn't want Ondrej to know how hopeless he felt sometimes.

"Perhaps, then, I'll take you up on your offer. It will give me something to do during the day if nothing else."

"Your unbridled enthusiasm is almost too much." Archie chuckled to show he was joking. He wasn't sure Ondrej really got his sense of humor.

Ondrej smiled, at least. "I *am* going to head home now, though. I went jogging in Central Park this morning and got horribly lost, and I'm starting to feel the extra distance I ran in order to get back." He shook out his arms. "Maybe I'll put something together for dinner. Or call in takeout. We should eat together. You're right, we should get to know each other to make our relationship more convincing."

That was something. "From what I've read, the green card process is fairly easy, but they might check up on us."

Ondrej grimaced. "I know."

"But I'll come home for dinner. We'll eat together. Yes?"

"Yes. Great. I'll see you tonight, then."

Ondrej left without even a hug or a kiss on the cheek, which was maybe too much to hope for. But dinner was a step in the right direction, and Archie was determined to think of it as such. Maybe he could salvage some of this mess and win Ondrej over.

Chapter Four

THE Katsaros offices took up three floors of a Sixth Avenue skyscraper, sharing the building with another big real estate office, a law firm, and a publishing company, among other businesses. The environment inside the building struck Ondrej as being rather formal, with everyone bustling around in suits and nicely coiffed hair. As he went through the security gate in the lobby, he watched a woman slide off her sneakers and step into a pair of very high red heels; he supposed she had to make the transition from subway traveler to office worker immediately upon entering the building.

Ondrej rode the elevator up to the eighth floor. Archie had the ability to zoom straight to the executive offices on ten, but one needed a special key card even to have the elevator doors open on that floor. Although now that Ondrej had an office there, he supposed he could talk to Marketa or someone about getting a magic key card. In the meantime, he had to settle for the same access everyone else at Katsaros had.

He intended to take the stairs that led from the accounts payable cube farm up to the offices on the ninth floor so he could swing by the kitchen, which had one of those fancy pod coffee machines, but he got waylaid when Archie himself suddenly came tearing through the office.

Archie was not exactly a small man. He was tall, nearly six two, with broad shoulders. His open suit jacket billowed behind him like a cape as he moved through the office. Several people gasped or jumped out of the way.

He didn't seem to see Ondrej, which was just as well.

Instead, he stopped near one of the copy machines and said, "I need everyone's attention."

He had it. No one had spoken since he'd first begun to plow through the rows of cubicles.

"There's a lot of shoddy, unacceptable work getting approved. I've had three expense reports come across my desk just today that had errors on them. Everyone, do better. Supervisors, check the math."

He blustered on for another minute or two about how everyone had to do their part to ensure the smooth running success of the company, which even Ondrej knew was mostly a façade. Surely these people knew that as well.

A short woman stood to Ondrej's left. "You're the new husband, aren't you?"

Ondrej nodded.

The woman sniffed. "Good luck with that."

Ondrej wanted to be offended, but she had a point. Archie was terrifying when he lost his temper.

He snarled and stomped around like a bull getting ready to charge.

Ondrej recognized it as bullshit alpha posturing, and it didn't intimidate him so much as irked him that Archie thought this was an effective way to manage employees.

On the other hand, the bullshit alpha stuff was kind of hot. Though Archie seemed to be losing his mind, Ondrej couldn't help but think about what would happen if Archie channeled all that passion into sex. How explosive that would be. Ondrej's skin went flush at the thought. He crossed his arms and took a step back from the woman next to him, suppressing the mental image.

Archie grumbled and turned toward Ondrej. He started, probably only just realizing Ondrej had witnessed that whole big ball of angry executive. He walked toward Ondrej with his shoulders up and his back straight, as if he were still stiffly putting on airs.

"Well, I suppose you think—" Archie started to say.

"I'm gonna get a cup of coffee. You want some?"

Archie frowned. "No, I'm fine."

"Are you sure? The french roast is really good."

"Are you here to work or to mooch off the coffee machine?"

"Some of both."

Archie pursed his lips. "All right. I'm going upstairs. I suppose I'll see you up there."

Archie blew past Ondrej and down the hall toward the receptionist, likely to take the elevator up to his floor so as to bypass the stairs all the little ants who worked for him used. Ondrej didn't know what to make of all this beyond wondering how much of what he'd just witnessed was real or just Archie getting mad. Was he always as gruff and angry as this little show indicated, or was this a rare moment of his losing it? And what did it say about Ondrej that he thought the whole thing was ridiculous and over-the-top, but he was more drawn to Archie than ever?

ARCHIE sat at his desk, mortified. He massaged his temples and leaned forward in such a way as to put his flooding e-mail in-box temporarily out of his line of sight. His heart pounded, his hands shook, and he thought not for the first time that he was probably not really cut out for the role of CEO of a major company, at least not the way his father had run it.

Because there was no way Alexander Katsaros would have tolerated the sloppiness Archie had seen in the reports submitted to him for final approval. One report, on expenses for the last month, was particularly heinous, littered with math errors. After Archie had crunched the numbers himself, he found out that the department had actually paid out nearly $3,000 more than the final tally in the report indicated. That was, if any of the figures in the report were reliable to begin with, which he wasn't completely confident about. Which meant the company was slowly bleeding money.

He'd done the math and then wondered what his father would have done. Well, his father would have stormed down there to yell and posture, and then everyone would have complied, because the elder Katsaros ran a tight ship. Archie mostly felt like the lookout man in the bird's nest of a huge ship, flailing about a distant iceberg.

That Ondrej had been there to witness it had completed Archie's humiliation. He was a poor leader compared to his father. Ondrej had seen his subpar attempts to whip his employees into shape.

God. Archie missed his father. He missed having the man around to show him the way, missed the feeling of security his father had created. He missed his father, period; they would never again cut out of work early to catch a baseball game or joke around in one of the conference rooms while drinking coffee and working on plans for the next fiscal year—they'd never even speak to each other again. He'd left a pretty big hole in Archie's life, one that seemed to be filling with doubt and insecurity.

Archie took a deep breath and tried to pull himself together. Ondrej appeared at his door a few minutes later with a paper coffee cup cradled in his hands. "Glad you got that out of your system?"

Archie felt worse, if that was even possible. "Half of why we're losing money is that no one in the whole damned department can do math," he said. "You should see these reports."

"You need more oversight. You can't do it all yourself."

"With what money can I hire new personnel? I can barely pay the people I have. And weren't you the one who just told me to lay people off?"

"What about the executive board?"

"They only care about the bottom line. Most of them only come into this office for meetings. They can't or won't do the day-to-day work needed to clean up this mess."

"All right, but wouldn't it be in their financial best interest to get more involved with the day-to-day?"

Perhaps, but Archie felt stuck between not wanting to give up control over the company for which he was still the majority shareholder and not wanting to let the board know just how bad the situation was. He wanted to get things under control before he brought the larger issues to the board. And anyway, Dan Preston—not coincidentally a distant cousin of Archie's on his mother's side—was the only board member who regularly put in time at the office. Dan was aware of the situation, mostly, and was the board member most fervently in favor of selling off the company. But Archie fought him because he couldn't see giving up such a significant part of his father's legacy.

The argument with Ondrej went in circles for a few minutes. Archie didn't like the meddling, even though he had essentially given Ondrej carte blanche to meddle by giving him the partnership. He was working up to a good "How dare you tell me how to run my business!" speech when Ondrej waved his hands and said, "Never mind. Run this sinking ship the way you want to."

That sucked all the wind out of Archie's sails. "You're implying the way I'm managing the company is responsible for the inefficiencies? Not the employees?"

"Yes, actually."

"But my father—"

"Look where that got him."

It was a fair point. But everyone had always gone on about what an effective leader Alexander Katsaros was. He'd built this real estate empire from almost nothing! He was domineering, yes, but he was also friendly and charming, a good family man, and by all accounts, everyone liked him. He'd made some poor investments toward the end of his life—that was clear from the bottom line—but he'd been effectively leading the company for a long time before that.

Archie was just picking up the reins in his stead. And he was falling far short of ever being as good at this as his father.

But he didn't want Ondrej to see how much of a failure he was, so as calmly as he could, he said, "I know I gave you some discretion, but I've been working here since I was a teenager. You were an intern for three months. You can't say with any authority what will or won't work in my company. I agreed to let you have a say in how we manage your money and what that money is spent on, but beyond that, you can't just impose your will. I'm still in charge."

He knew he sounded like a petulant child, but Archie tried to deliver the speech with as much bravado as he could muster. Because in the end, this was his company. Because he was running it. He might not always feel confident in his decisions, but they were his to make.

"Fine," said Ondrej. "It's yours. I was merely offering a suggestion. Maybe a hard line worked in the past, but that's not the way the world works anymore, and I believe you would do well to change your attitude. Shouting doesn't accomplish anything beyond making your employees afraid of you."

"Maybe that's what I want."

Ondrej's eyes went wide. "Well, sure. It's a way to do business."

That seemed to effectively end the conversation, much to Archie's consternation. He knew he was going about this all wrong. If the real goal was to win over Ondrej so that they had a shot at some kind of relationship—something Archie still wanted despite Ondrej acting like kind of a know-it-all now—he had to stop antagonizing Ondrej.

Because Archie just couldn't picture sharing his house with a man who continued to put distance between them. The only way to make this work and keep his sanity was to forge a relationship, even just a friendship, with Ondrej. But Archie still wanted Ondrej, still felt every cell pulling toward Ondrej when he was near. This distance was torture, and he hoped to close it soon.

"Why are you in the office?" he tried to ask as neutrally as possible. "Not just to steal coffee."

"No. I wanted to take a look at those financial reports you gave me access to, plus I was feeling bored at home. There are only so many walks around the neighborhood one can take, you know?"

"All right. Let me know if you have questions about any of it."

"I will." Ondrej stood.

"I'm not selling my company."

"I know. I won't bother to argue why you should. The company is your livelihood. I get that. I'm not even sure selling the whole thing is the best solution to the problem."

"All right. But know that some board members do think selling at least part of the company is the best solution."

"It may not come to that. Hopefully it won't." Ondrej sighed and placed a hand on top of the chair he'd just vacated. "I didn't intend to pick a fight when I came here today."

"No, I know. It's fine. We just disagree."

"Right." Ondrej nodded and left the room.

Archie felt like he'd just shoved his whole foot in his mouth.

Chapter Five

WHEN Archie came home a few nights later, he found Ondrej curled up on the sofa in the den, watching TV.

Archie had been simmering in sexual frustration ever since Ondrej had claimed his office at Katsaros Holdings. They hadn't spoken much, either at home or at the office, but having Ondrej around more had put Archie's body on red alert. He was constantly aware that Ondrej was nearby, even if he wasn't visible. When they did speak to each other, it was mostly in one of their offices with the doors closed, and they'd sit close and go over computer files or printouts, and Archie was half out of his mind because he wanted to toss the facts and figures aside and rip Ondrej's clothes off.

So he stood in the doorway to the den, watching Ondrej for a moment as Ondrej flipped through the channels.

"I really am attracted to you, you know," Archie said.

Ondrej turned and looked at him, raising an eyebrow. "Are you?"

"Half the reason I agreed to this whole scheme is I think you're sexy. I thought, 'Hell, I'm attracted to him. I won't have to fake that, at least.'"

Ondrej shifted his weight on the sofa until he was sitting up straight. "What are you saying?"

"Forget it." Archie figured his affections weren't returned, which was usually how this went.

"No, I don't want to forget it. Are you saying you want something to happen between us?"

Archie couldn't read Ondrej's expression and didn't want to risk too much. "If you want to. I mean, we're stuck in this situation for a while."

Ondrej smiled. "Well, that's an enthusiastic proposal. Might as well, right?"

Disgusted with himself now, Archie waved his hands. "Seriously, forget it. We'll just go to our separate rooms tonight and pretend we're not married."

Ondrej stood and slowly walked toward where Archie stood in the doorway. "We agreed to get married because it seemed plausible. I know that's not romantic, but…." Ondrej stepped closer, within touching distance of Archie. "I'm attracted to you too."

Ondrej closed the distance between them and softly pressed his lips against Archie's. Archie sighed and deepened the kiss. It was what he wanted, what he'd been hoping for, but the reality was so much better than what he imagined. Ondrej's mouth was hot and wet and perfect.

But before Archie could really savor the kiss, Ondrej pulled away again. "We still barely know each other. Normally that wouldn't be an obstacle for me to get naked with someone, but I still have to live with you. Maybe we could think it over, decide what we want, take it slow. What do you think?"

Archie thought he wanted to keep kissing Ondrej. He wanted to throw Ondrej on his sofa and ravish him. He wanted Ondrej's legs wrapped around his waist, wanted to be naked and sweaty on the floor, wanted anything but this strained distance between them. But he said, "Yeah, you're probably right." Then he remembered his real purpose for coming into the room. "By the way, we've been invited to a charity gala on Friday. It's to be our first public appearance as a couple."

Ondrej laughed softly. "All right. What's the charity?"

"Literacy, I think. It doesn't matter. The way these things work is we pay an exorbitant amount of money to have a small dinner and schmooze with the One Percent. Marketa thinks this is a great opportunity to be seen together publicly and make the marriage look legit."

"Is it formal?"

"Yes. Do you own a tux?"

"No, but I can get one by Friday. Is there a reason you're talking about this as if you're about to go before a firing squad?"

Archie let out a breath. "Because it feels that way. I'm worried no one will buy us as a couple. How good of an actor are you?"

Ondrej smirked. "I can pretend with the best of them. We'll be all right. At least we know we're not repulsed by each other. We won't have to fake an attraction."

"Yeah?" Archie was distracted by Ondrej's proximity, by his dark, tousled hair and his soft-looking skin.

"Yeah. Can you act?"

"I've been going to parties like this my whole life. What do you think?"

Ondrej grinned. "See? No one will be the wiser."

Archie nodded and then figured he should get out of the room before he embarrassed himself. "Well, I'm just going to find something for dinner. You okay?"

"Already ate. There's some leftover lasagna from that Italian place on Eighty-Second, if you want it."

When Archie turned to leave, Ondrej grabbed his arm and kissed his cheek. He looked over Ondrej with a question burning in his brain. But Ondrej just smiled. "I think I may have misjudged you," Ondrej said.

"How so?"

Ondrej stepped back and shrugged. "Go eat dinner. We'll talk later."

With that, Ondrej drifted back to the sofa and resumed watching TV. Archie went into the kitchen, wondering what had just happened to him.

It had been so long since he'd kissed anybody. Archie'd had his fair amount of casual sex in his twenties, when the spotlight wasn't shining on him so glaringly, but since his father's health had started failing, he hadn't gone out much. He worked most days well into the night. He hadn't chosen celibacy, exactly, but the days without any sort of companionship had turned into weeks, then months, and now it had been about a year. He'd grown accustomed to his solitude, but now that Ondrej was in the house and just out of reach, Archie felt only longing and frustration.

Archie hadn't realized how lonely he was until he had Ondrej around to remind him.

He put the leftovers in the oven and mused that he had someone looking out for him besides just Hildy, which was kind of nice. The kitchen quickly filled with the smell of warming marinara sauce and melting cheese, and Archie smiled to himself. The situation with Ondrej was crazy-making, no doubt, but the kiss had felt like a promise.

AS Ondrej was falling asleep that night, he put his fingers to his lips and realized he wanted to kiss Archie again. He wanted to do some other things with Archie, but what he really wanted was the sweet affection from that kiss downstairs, not a sexy ravishment as he'd been picturing since the wedding.

So this would be slow going.

The weird thing was that, if nothing else, the past couple of days had shown Ondrej that perhaps Archie was not the tyrant his employees so frequently painted him as. He seemed out of place in this dramatic house, even, like his true desires were much simpler than crystal chandeliers and damask curtains. His desire to fix the company without anyone losing their jobs was charmingly naive but showed he cared about his employees.

Was it an act?

Ondrej was starting to think Archie took a hard-line approach to his public persona in order to appear to be something he wasn't. And that was interesting.

Ondrej rolled onto his side and thought about what it would be like to be lying next to Archie in bed instead of sprawling across this queen-size mattress by himself. He thought not so much about what Archie would be like in bed—likely a conscientious lover, if his behavior recently was any indicator—but about whether Archie liked touching his partner as he slept, if he snored, if he tended to curl up in the fetal position at night.

It was a weird line of thinking.

Ondrej had spent his first month in New York working by day and then slipping into the New York gay club scene at night, going home with whoever would have him and often waking up and having to figure out how to get from a neighborhood he didn't know to the Katsaros offices in the morning. That had all dried up the day his boss, Amy, had introduced him to Archie.

Ondrej had been instantly attracted, sure. He hadn't intended to act on that attraction—Archie was still in a superior position—but Archie had something arresting about him. And, truthfully, Ondrej had a few ways out of his predicament that would have been less costly. He could have gotten a more menial job or another low-paying internship in order to renew his work visa. He probably could have thrown money at the problem and hired a top-notch lawyer to sort through everything. But he'd spent enough time looking at Archie by the time Marketa had called him into that conference room meeting, and when it became clear that they could help each other out, somehow a lifelong romantic commitment had seemed like an easier option.

The whole process that had led to this point was utterly insane. But clearly Ondrej had seen something in Archie he'd wanted to explore. But now that he was in the thick of this situation, he felt like he needed to tread more carefully. He was terrified things with Archie would go horribly wrong, and he was reluctant to shake up the status quo.

But was living a celibate life in a fading mansion really what he wanted to stay in America for?

He fell asleep that night thinking it might be worth it if he pursued Archie for real. He faced real risk there; what if it turned out they were totally incompatible or had a vicious fight? Would Archie kick him out? Would he be able to find a job or some other means of staying in the US? Would he have to go back to his family?

And could they even pull off this fraud? Could they convince whatever press showed up at the gala that they were crazy in love?

Ondrej wasn't sure about any of it, but if he was going to make the most of the opportunity he'd been given, he'd have to pursue it somehow.

Chapter Six

ONDREJ ensconced himself on the sofa in the den.
The AC was on high, how Archie liked it most of
the time, so Ondrej had wrapped a blanket around
himself and leaned into the cushions. He was
comfortable, which was what he needed, because he
was about to make a phone call he very much did not
want to make.

But he dialed.

And his mother answered.

"Oh, Ondrej, darling. Are you still in New York?
Your visa must have expired." She said all this in rapid
Czech, her tone a little belligerent.

"I have something to tell you."

"When are you coming home?"

"I'm not."

A long silence passed before she spoke. "What do you mean you're not? You can't stay in America forever."

"I can, actually. I've applied for a green card."

"On what basis? Are you moving permanently? I thought you lost your job."

Ondrej took a deep breath. "I did lose my job. But I got married."

She gasped so loud all of Eastern Europe probably heard it. "You did not. What is this getting married nonsense? You can't just get married."

"Well, I did." He took a deep breath. "I'm in love."

"How could you get married? Without inviting me? Who is the woman?"

"It's not a woman, Ma. I'm gay, remember? I married a man."

She shrieked in such a high octave Ondrej had to jerk the phone away from his ear to avoid going deaf. "Ondrej! How could you do this to me?"

Ondrej sighed. "I didn't do it *to* you. I did it for myself. I fell in love with someone and we got married so that I can stay here and live with him." There. That was close enough to the truth.

She yelled and ranted for nearly a minute before she took a deep breath and said, "It's one thing for you to get married without telling me. I am disappointed, and I would have liked to come to your wedding."

"It wasn't much of a wedding. We eloped."

"Do not interrupt me. I haven't finished. I am disappointed you hid this from me. But I am more disappointed that you would so publicly display your perversion by marrying a man."

"It's not—"

"It's a good thing you have a home in America now, because you are no longer welcome here."

With that she hung up.

It was essentially the response Ondrej had expected, but he hadn't anticipated the sadness that swept over him and the strange hollow feeling in his gut. She'd just confirmed what he'd suspected all along: that he was her son, but only if he behaved in ways she found acceptable. Such had been the way of his childhood. It was why he'd moved to France to live with his grandparents after he'd dropped out of school. Hell, it was why he'd moved to America to begin with.

It was only after he'd been staring at the phone for a minute that he realized his mother hadn't even asked about his new husband; she hadn't asked what he did for a living or whether he was a good man or even his name. That he was male was all the information she had needed to pronounce her judgment and tell Ondrej he was not welcome at home any longer.

He took a deep breath and tried to get his heartbeat back to normal. He'd call his father later to make amends, but he didn't have the energy for it now.

Archie came into the room. Ondrej hadn't even heard him come home.

"It's cold in here," Archie commented. "I guess I can let up on the AC now that it's definitely fall."

Ondrej huddled under the blanket.

Archie walked over to the thermostat and adjusted it. When he turned back to the couch, he paused for a moment and then said, "Are you okay?"

"Just told my mother I married a man. She said not to come home." The words came out flat. Ondrej couldn't make himself lift his head to look at Archie.

"Oh, no. Oh, Ondrej."

The speed with which Archie sat on the couch and pulled Ondrej into his arms surprised Ondrej. Still, he welcomed the hug and snaked his arms out from under the blanket to hug Archie back. The hollow feeling grew; he'd been abandoned, exiled. He'd come here to get away from his mother's judgment, but he felt it just the same, and he had the niggling sense that this marriage trick was not going to solve anything.

"It's not so bad," Ondrej said, trying to cheer himself up.

Archie rocked him a little. "It's never easy to get rejected by your parents."

"No, but… I expected this. It's why it took me so long to call home."

"Still. I know how awful you must feel. I wish I could take that away."

So Ondrej tucked his head under Archie's chin and sympathized with Archie too, because he imagined that there was some point when Archie's hero father had told Archie he wasn't good enough. Whether his deficiencies were due to a lack of leadership skill or his homosexuality, Ondrej couldn't have known, but it almost didn't matter. He knew Archie understood this rejection, had known this hollow sensation himself. Archie probably knew the loneliness of feeling like one had no allies. So Ondrej said nothing more; he merely let Archie hug him.

"We're in this together, you know," Archie said.

"Hmm?"

Archie rubbed Ondrej's arms. "We made an agreement. The two of us are in this situation together, working toward the same goal. You're not alone. If you need someone to talk to, I'm here."

Ondrej inhaled deeply, taking in the faint minty scent of whatever cologne or aftershave Archie used. "You're doing enough right now."

"Good. But for future reference."

"Yes. Thank you."

Archie's compassion was so out of place with the man Ondrej had come to know in the weeks he'd been in the Katsaros office. Even at home, he wasn't as gruff and angry, but he was often cold and distant. This Archie, the one holding Ondrej in his strong arms, occasionally petting his hair... this Archie was warm and affectionate. Which was the real Archie? Ondrej hoped it was the latter, because as he nuzzled against Archie's shoulder, this Archie gave him comfort.

AS Archie got in bed that night, he wondered what was happening and how he'd misunderstood the situation before him. Seeing Ondrej so out of sorts had thrown him off guard. Ondrej was always so stoic; seeing him vulnerable had undone something in Archie.

He pulled back the covers and imagined what it would be like to have Ondrej with him in this big bed. He'd wanted it since first agreeing to the marriage scheme, though he'd held it out as a distant hope, since Ondrej didn't seem interested. But what if Ondrej had more to him than what he showed on the surface? He was so flippant about everything, but his mother's rejection had really hurt him.

So Archie had done his best to comfort Ondrej and had even considered inviting him to the big bed tonight, but something about that felt predatory. He didn't want to take advantage of Ondrej's vulnerability. No, when Ondrej came to Archie in the night, Archie wanted it to be of his own volition.

So perhaps he was approaching the situation incorrectly. Archie had been content to take a more passive role in their relationship, letting Ondrej dictate the terms, but maybe he should be more aggressive.

He thought back to something Ondrej had said in the office about the way Archie dealt with the employees. Perhaps Archie losing his patience was not the best way to deal with the people who worked under him; perhaps Alexander Katsaros's way of dealing with things didn't work for Archie, or didn't work in the modern business environment.

So maybe it was time for Archie to change his approach to all of it.

Funny how his personal life required aggressive behavior but his work life required a gentler touch.

Archie pulled his covers up over him and let out a breath as he settled into the bed. As he drifted off to sleep, he was still thinking about how to handle both his business and his husband.

Chapter Seven

ARCHIE stood in the foyer, tugging on his cuffs, hoping the tux really fit. It was a few years old, and he'd lost some weight in the past few months. Stress had a way of forcing one to worry off the pounds.

Archie pushed all that out of his mind, though. Instead, he looked around him and thought of every movie where the heroine descended the grand staircase, transformed by a spectacular dress and a little makeup, and the hero finally understood what she was all about. Of course, Archie's hero wouldn't be descending the staircase in a ball gown, and though Archie was confident his husband would look fantastic, he was less sure there was a happy ending in store for them.

But a moment later, descend the staircase Ondrej did, resplendent in a very expensive-looking tuxedo that was remarkably well cut to his figure considering he'd had little time to get it tailored. His tie was an interesting black-and-tan check that looked good near his olive skin. Ondrej's hair was slicked out of his face, making him look that much more handsome.

Archie imagined he looked like a cartoon character with his tongue hanging out and his heart beating out of his chest as he watched Ondrej approach.

Ondrej smiled, which really did send flutters through Archie's chest. As Ondrej reached the bottom of the staircase, Archie held out his arm. Ondrej slipped his hand around Archie's elbow and they walked that way to the door, neither of them speaking.

In fact, it wasn't until they were in the back of the car Archie had hired to take them to the gala that either spoke, and then it was Ondrej to say, "You look nice."

Archie grinned. He couldn't help it. "This old thing?"

Ondrej chuckled as he reached over to straighten Archie's tie. "I like this purple," he said, running his hand over the tie. "You should wear more color. Your wardrobe is so bland."

"Gee, thanks."

"No, I didn't mean that as an insult. I just meant your wardrobe is conservative, perhaps as fits a CEO of a major company, but I think you'd look wonderful if you wore a little more color. It would make you stand out more."

"I'll keep that in mind."

Archie was enjoying the gentle touches of Ondrej's fingers near his neck and chest, but Ondrej withdrew his hands. "I don't really understand this New Yorker preoccupation with black. Everyone is always dressed like they're on the way to a funeral."

"Hard to go wrong with a classic," said Archie.

Ondrej smiled softly again. "You are a handsome man, Archie. Perhaps I haven't been free with compliments, but I assumed this was something you already heard a lot."

"Not as much as you'd think." Archie glanced out the window and calculated they were about three blocks from their destination. "Are you ready for this?"

"As I'll ever be."

This was an invitation-only gala at a hotel ballroom in Midtown, where Archie knew from experience the main object was to be seen. Some charity always benefitted from the magnanimous guests, of course, but New York society would turn out at these things to get their pictures taken more than to donate the money. Archie admonished himself for being so cynical, but he'd been in this world a long time.

The car pulled up to the hotel, and as discussed, Archie got out first and helped Ondrej out of the car. Ondrej leaned close and whispered, "Time to pretend you're the love of my life."

Archie nodded, but it occurred to him he wouldn't have to pretend very hard.

Ondrej walked alongside Archie into the hotel lobby, where they were met by a liveried attendant who said, "Right this way, Mr. Katsaros," and led them to the ballroom. The room was already packed with well-dressed people milling about. Archie spotted Cathleen Brandt, whom he'd gone to school with but who was now largely considered an aging socialite, probably here on the prowl for a third husband. He spotted a former Katsaros employee who had created his own real estate empire a few years ago and was by all accounts absurdly successful. And, oh, over there in the corner was the mayor of New York City, talking to a Broadway actor and a magazine editor.

"Some party," Ondrej said. "I could get lost here."

"Stick with me," Archie said, because he needed support suddenly. He'd done dozens of these parties before, but he felt overwhelmed and out of his element. The elder Katsaros had been the master of putting on a good face for the public. Archie had always been content to follow his father's lead or else fade into the background.

Archie reached back, and Ondrej slid his hand into Archie's.

"You're out to this crowd, right?" Ondrej asked.

"Yes. Well, I brought a male date to the last one of these events. And our wedding was announced in the *Times*, remember?"

"Yes, right. I'm still getting the hang of all this. The guests at this gala would have seen the announcement?"

"I don't know how many of them browse the wedding announcements, but we've likely been discussed among certain circles." Archie squeezed Ondrej's hand. "You grew up with a certain amount of wealth and privilege, did you not? This can't all be new to you."

"No, but you Americans have a distinct way of doing things." Ondrej took a deep breath. "That, and I cannot imagine my family would have permitted me to attend a swanky party with a male date."

"Good thing you're in America, then. With your husband."

"Husband. Lord, that still seems strange."

Archie nodded, but he knew perfectly well that a lot of the strangeness came from their barely even being in a relationship, hand-holding notwithstanding. With time, that would go away.

Although how much time they had was an open question.

"Mr. Katsaros!"

Archie turned his head and saw Priscilla Zimmer, who wrote a gossipy society column, marching toward him.

"Here's the first test," he said to Ondrej.

When Priscilla reached them, she smiled and said, "Well, Archie, how are you?"

"I am fantastic." Archie glanced at Ondrej, who was still holding his hand. "Allow me to introduce my new husband, Ondrej Kovac."

Ondrej smiled and held out his other hand.

Priscilla shook it and said, "Congratulations! I hadn't heard you'd gotten married."

Archie sighed. "Of course you did, or you wouldn't have walked over here." He turned to Ondrej. "Darling, this is Priscilla Zimmer. She writes for the *Post*."

Priscilla smiled. "Actually, I have my own website now. I reach more readers that way. No one reads papers anymore." She turned toward Ondrej. "So, tell me all your secrets. How did you meet?"

They had discussed and rehearsed this, knowing there would likely be reporters and/or gossip columnists about, and Ondrej plastered on a smile and said his lines perfectly. "Funny story. I interned at Katsaros Holdings this summer. I know it sounds inappropriate, but we spotted each other across the crowded office floor and it was love at first sight." He squeezed Archie's hand and then looked at him adoringly.

Archie knew it was an act, but he felt that flutter again. He couldn't keep from smiling back. "It's been a whirlwind."

"I couldn't help but notice your accent," said Priscilla. "Where are you from?"

"The Czech Republic. Just outside Prague. Hence the internship. I had no work experience in the US, but I went to business school and worked for my family for many years, so it's not like I'm fresh out of university."

Priscilla grinned like a cat who'd caught a mouse. "So, a visitor to the US gets a job at one of the biggest real estate firms in New York and just happens to fall in love with the owner. That's quite an upgrade!"

Archie saw the comment as the insult it was, implying Ondrej was a gold digger, but Ondrej just smiled. "Well, just last summer, I sold the winery owned by my grandparents for a healthy profit. I have no interest in Archie's money, since I have plenty of my own. We really did fall for each other this summer."

Ondrej gave Archie another adoring smile. Archie had trouble catching his breath for a moment.

And, of course, Priscilla wouldn't catch on that the situation was actually reversed—that Archie needed Ondrej for his money.

"My, my," said Priscilla. She turned her attention to Archie. "So, tell me something else, sweetheart. The new Brooklyn Eagles stadium project. Someone is finally going to tear down that rusty old baseball stadium?"

"We're just waiting on some paperwork for the city, but if all goes to plan, construction will begin in the spring."

"And affordable housing is part of your plan."

"Yes."

Priscilla knew full well the law required any developments on the scale of the Eagles stadium project to include a certain percentage of affordable apartments.

That had always been part of the plan. Archie had high hopes that development would revive an otherwise waning neighborhood; the existing stadium was sandwiched between Prospect Park and a neglected patch of Brooklyn full of failing schools and crumbling old buildings.

But it was a long-term investment, since they hadn't even broken ground yet, and it wasn't one he'd talked about with Ondrej, so he wished Priscilla would change the subject.

"Well, you're certainly a very attractive couple," Priscilla said. "Congrats on the nuptials. I see my friend Susie over there, so I'll talk to you later. Ta-ta!"

When she was gone, Ondrej dropped Archie's hand and said, "A lot just happened there."

"She reports on society. I've met her a handful of times before."

"Right. I got that. When were you planning to tell me about the Eagles stadium project? I thought it was on hold."

Archie sighed and pinched the bridge of his nose. "Can we not talk about this now? I think if we had a big argument in the middle of this ballroom, people might suspect all is not wonderful in marital paradise."

Ondrej took a deep breath and nodded. "All right. Tomorrow, then. But I don't like you holding a secret about the company like that from me, especially if you're bringing me on as a partner. And if a reporter already knows about it, I look like a fool for not being kept in the loop."

"I understand that. We'll talk tomorrow, I promise."

A waiter walked by with a tray of hors d'oeuvres. Archie snagged a little pastry, not even caring what it was. It tasted like cardboard anyway. He wanted Ondrej's hand back.

Instead, he gestured toward the bar. Ondrej followed. As they ordered wine and waited, Cathleen Brandt walked over.

"I saw your announcement in the *Times*," Cathleen said as she kissed Archie's cheeks. "This must be the new husband."

Archie put his hand on the small of Ondrej's back and nudged him forward a little. "This is Ondrej." He turned to Ondrej. "This is Cathleen, an old school friend."

They shook hands. Ondrej stayed silent.

"You know," said Cathleen, "I had quite forgotten you were gay before I read the announcement. But then I remembered you spent a good portion of ninth grade sneaking around with Joel Cooper. Not at all subtly, I might add. I think the whole school was onto you."

Archie held back a physical reaction to the memory. Hearing Cathleen talk about it so frankly bothered him, though he wasn't sure why; it wasn't like he was trying to hide anything now. Perhaps he was still adjusting to not having to play coy around his father. So he grinned. After all, he had some fond memories of Joel Cooper. "I wouldn't have cared if the whole school knew, as long as my parents didn't."

Cathleen frowned. "I heard about your father. I'm so sorry for your loss."

"Thank you. It's been a strange few months."

Archie wished Ondrej would speak now. Likely Ondrej was contemplating the Eagles stadium deal, but there was nothing to be done about it here. Archie felt awkward, lacking his father's gift for charming a crowd, but if Ondrej were more engaged, this might feel smoother. He glanced at Ondrej, who stood there smiling placidly and gazing at the people in the ballroom.

"Well, this must have been some romance," said Cathleen. "Was there a wedding?"

"We eloped. We didn't want anything big or ostentatious."

"Or even a honeymoon," said Ondrej. Finally. "Too tied up with work."

"That's sad," said Cathleen.

"It is sad," Ondrej said, coming back to himself and looping his hand around Archie's arm. "We've been married about two weeks and have done nothing to celebrate. What about that trip to the Florida Keys?"

"That can still be arranged," said Archie, playing along. He was pretty sure they both knew there would be no trip.

"Of course, darling. No rush. We just got married. We have the whole rest of our lives!"

And wasn't that a daunting prospect?

"Well, you make an adorable couple," Cathleen said. "I'll admit, I was a little surprised to see the announcement. But as long as you're happy, that's what's important."

"We're *very* happy," Ondrej said, patting Archie's chest. "Dearest, I believe our wine is ready."

AFTER Cathleen left, Ondrej kept his hand wrapped around Archie's upper arm because he couldn't quite make himself let go. Touching Archie made him seem... corporeal. Human. Masculine. The long line of Archie's bicep under Ondrej's palm reminded him suddenly that Archie was a man, and a sexy one, and not just a cardboard cutout boss or his pretend husband.

"Do you do this sort of thing often?" Ondrej asked. "Everyone here seems to know you."

"I attended a lot of these kinds of events with my father after I went to work for him. I hated this kind of stuff. I was always more of a wallflower, but he had a real facility with people and crowds. He could charm the socks off anyone. I was just his awkward son. I had to get over myself and start doing these functions after he got sick."

"I doubt there's an awkward bone in your body."

Archie smiled faintly. "Kind of you to say, but a lot of this is just acting and practice. Inside, I hate this and I'm terrified. Having to show you off is only making it worse."

Ondrej couldn't respond before his thoughts were drowned out by a commotion on one side of the room. A small crowd of people clapped as a band took up a few chairs in the corner of the room. They began playing soft jazz.

"This is the part of the evening," Archie said, "where everyone will stand around gawking and talking about how good the band is for about a half hour, and then someone will cajole Mrs. Mortimer to talk her recalcitrant husband into dancing with her, and then everyone over fifty will join them for a waltz, and then the younger folk start dancing too. But this is a classy party, so no bumping and grinding, and the band won't play anything faster than a foxtrot or more modern than Duke Ellington."

Ondrej wasn't entirely sure what all that meant, but he nodded.

"This was really more my mother's world," Archie said. "Her family has been attending balls like this since the Gilded Age, and you'd think it would be in my blood or something, but it isn't quite."

Ondrej sipped his wine and gazed around the ballroom. His family had means, it was true, though he'd been born toward the end of the Cold War, when things in Prague were not so peachy. He'd been oblivious to a lot of it, but he grew up with a sense of tension in the house, of things not always being safe or secure. He'd learned later that a great deal of his family's success came from doing business with the USSR, but even that had a fragile base. That they'd thrived for the past twenty years still seemed remarkable.

Of course, they'd traveled. Ondrej's grandmother had moved to France to run a successful winery. Ondrej had sold it shortly after her death, invested the money, and now lived off the profits. He wondered if his grandmother would roil at the prospect of his using the money to bail out a company that made most of its money building apartment complexes and sports stadiums in already overcrowded neighborhoods.

That Eagles stadium project was a disaster waiting to happen.

But Ondrej had agreed to put it aside for now, so, after promising himself he would bring it up with Archie in the morning, he pushed it out of his mind.

He stared instead at the opulence of this party and thought of a few similar galas he'd attended in France with his grandmother when he was quite young. They'd had that same sense of expectation and rhythm, of doing things the same way for two hundred years and deliberately not explaining to exclude anyone new or from too far outside the inner circle of wealth and privilege. Ondrej had attended fancy French parties at the winery or in Lyon or Paris. In the nineties, there had been fancy parties in Prague too, once the government was no longer run by people who wanted to stamp out creativity and development.

But that was all in the past, part of the complicated history Ondrej had tried to escape by coming to New York. Yet here he was, sipping wine in a ballroom not so different from ballrooms back home.

At least Archie hated this as much as Ondrej did.

They spent the next half hour schmoozing with various people Archie knew—many of whom had last names even Ondrej recognized—and, as predicted, the older couples started dancing. It was all very chaste and formal, like something out of another era.

"Do you think this crowd is scandalized by us?" Ondrej asked.

"What do you mean?" Archie placed his empty wineglass on a tray as a waiter walked by with it. "Because we're a gay couple?"

"Prague is a fairly progressive city, but the high society parties are so stuffy and conservative. And if my parents were there…."

"Good thing we're not in Prague." Archie tilted his head. "I think fifteen years ago, we would have had a few blue-haired ladies saying, 'Well, I never!' but less so now. Jessica Mortimer brings female dates to things all the time."

"Is that a name I should know?"

"She's the redhead over by that podium over there. She's the dictionary definition of a socialite. Vanderbilt descendant, if I remember correctly. A favorite of the tabloids because she's beautiful and lesbian and is frequently attending events where she knows there will be lots of cameras."

"So a gay couple in an allegedly committed relationship shouldn't turn any heads."

"It might turn a few, but I don't think anyone will give us any trouble." Archie turned and looked at Ondrej directly. "What do you mean by 'allegedly'? I know the circumstances are strange, but I'm committed."

Ondrej turned that over in his mind and realized that he too had committed, in a way. He hadn't slept with anyone else since the wedding and didn't plan to—it felt strange to even contemplate that when he was living in Archie's house. He hadn't thought through whether he could remain celibate until his green card was in hand, but if that was what it took to get one, he'd do it. On the other hand, a part of him had always assumed that he and Archie would sleep together eventually. So if fidelity was the cost of doing business, Ondrej would do it.

"I'm committed too," said Ondrej. "But we hadn't talked about it."

Archie nodded. "Glad we're on the same page."

It felt like the end of a business meeting.

A woman in her fifties wearing an ostentatious red ball gown walked out onto the dance floor with a microphone. After introducing herself as Patricia Barrow, a member of the executive board of the charity the gala was raising money for, she gave some speech about how she appreciated everyone's contributions for the cause.

Then she said, "I understand we have some newlyweds in the audience."

Ondrej's heart sank.

"I'm sure we were all delighted to hear that Alexander Katsaros's son has finally succumbed to the charms of matrimony." Ms. Barrow paced a little as she spoke. "Archimedes, please let us all meet your new spouse."

Archie grabbed Ondrej's hand and led him to the dance floor, so Ondrej forced a smile and waved at the crowd. This was his grand introduction to society, after all.

Patricia Barrow held out the microphone to Archie. He bashfully refused, waving his hand and shaking his head with a grin on his face, but after she insisted, he relented.

After sighing heavily, he held the microphone in front of his mouth. "I'm sure my father would have loved to be here. He loved coming to events like this, and he loved talking to people. It's a little strange to be here without him." Archie looked down, blinking rapidly a few times as if keeping back tears. Acting or real, Ondrej didn't know. A sympathetic murmur rose through the crowd. Archie looked up again and said, "Tonight, instead of Dad, I brought my husband, Ondrej Kovac." He gazed at Ondrej with what seemed like genuine affection. Now the murmur became happier. "I know this is a surprise to just about all of you. It was a surprise to me too. But I just… the first time I laid eyes on Ondrej, I knew."

For a second Ondrej believed him.

But it was a ruse. Ondrej played along; he smiled and squeezed Archie's hand. Their eyes met for a brief moment. It was a bit like being inside a romantic snow globe; nothing outside of their immediate sphere was important.

But then Patricia Barrow said, "That's so sweet."

Her tone was patronizing, and it bothered Ondrej enough to pull him out of the fantasy where he and Archie were real newlyweds, madly in love with each other.

"Dance!" someone from the crowd yelled.

Archie—who was clearly a gifted actor, betraying none of the discomfort he must have felt given that the virtual spotlight they were now under was making Ondrej sweat—said, "Well, we didn't really have much of a wedding reception, did we? Ondrej, will you dance with me?"

"I will," Ondrej said.

The band started up again. Archie handed the microphone to Patricia and then held out his arms. Ondrej knew he had to play along, so he stepped closer to Archie and let himself get pulled into a dance as the follower.

Archie had a large wingspan: a wide chest and long arms. He was in good shape—he left the office for about an hour to hit the gym a few afternoons a week—and he had a certain protectiveness about him. Ondrej felt slighter, flimsier; he was a hair shorter and a good forty pounds lighter than Archie. Archie's arms, in contrast to Ondrej's, were strong and stable. Ondrej felt safe in them, cared for.

He wasn't used to following when he danced, but Archie had clearly had some kind of training and was a masterful leader. Ondrej had to concentrate on doing the steps backward, but Archie knew exactly how to apply pressure with his hands and arms to get Ondrej to move in sync with him.

So Ondrej let himself be led, and he looked up and met Archie's powerful gaze. For a moment there was potential. It was fiery and intense, boxed-up passion, the sense that Ondrej could absolutely be with this man in every way possible if only they could tear down the flimsy barriers between them.

Because Archie was beautiful. He was complicated. He was polished and well-trained but also had a temper.

He was rebellious and clever. He didn't want this life but was determined to live it anyway. Ondrej was here for appearances, yes, but perhaps Archie needed him as more than just a prop or a source of money.

Perhaps Archie needed balance, affection, someone in his life to make everything make sense.

Other people joined in to dance around them, but Ondrej tried to ignore them. He wanted this feeling of really being with Archie to last. He wanted Archie's arms around him, wanted Archie's strength to protect him, wanted to burrow against that wide expanse of his chest and simply revel in their closeness.

The music built to a crescendo. Ondrej met Archie's gaze again. And then they were kissing.

Ondrej didn't know who initiated the kiss, but it didn't matter, because it was perfect. They were surrounded by people and designer ball gowns and jazz but it didn't matter because they were kissing and they had their arms wrapped around each other, and for one fleeting moment, this was everything.

And then it ended.

The music retreated, as did Archie. He stepped away from Ondrej as the song ended. And then they were mobbed. Strangers offered Ondrej their heartfelt congratulations and welcomes. Archie kept a hand on Ondrej through all of it, as if he too were afraid they'd be separated by the crowd and never find each other again. Ondrej looked at Archie and caught his gaze, but Archie only smiled and shrugged.

Maybe he hated this world, but he was good at playing in it.

And so was Ondrej, so he grinned and shook hands and hated himself a little for having to fake something that felt suddenly within his grasp.

Chapter Eight

WHEN they arrived back home, Archie let them into the house with a sigh.

"I know you're upset about the stadium project, but—"

"No," said Ondrej, moving in behind Archie, nudging him toward the staircase. He put his hand on Archie's shoulder and slid it toward his neck. "I'm okay with tabling it for now." He tugged on Archie until they were close enough to feel each other's breath. "I have something else on my mind right now." He kissed Archie.

Archie groaned. Ondrej's kiss was like a glass of water after a dry, thirsty afternoon.

Ondrej ran his hands through Archie's hair and pulled away slightly. "Take me to bed," he whispered.

"Yes," said Archie.

Archie's pulse raced with nervousness, because he wanted to get this right, but he also wanted to take advantage of the opportunity. He took both of Ondrej's hands in his and squeezed them. Then he hooked an arm around Ondrej's and led him up the stairs. On the way, Ondrej tripped on a step and laughed. It was a joyous sound, a good sound, a sound that indicated tonight had some magic in store.

Archie led Ondrej to his bedroom, where the big bed dominated the space. It had been made earlier in the day because Hildy had stopped by, giving the room the appearance that someone who kept things neat lived here. Not that it mattered, since they were about to mess it up.

Archie kissed Ondrej, slipping his tongue into Ondrej's mouth to taste him. He pulled Ondrej close and clawed at his clothes, wanting them off and away. He nudged Ondrej toward the bed. Ondrej grabbed at Archie too, sliding his hands under Archie's shirt and the waistband of his pants and pawing at his skin.

"Off," Archie muttered against Ondrej's lips.

Ondrej must have understood, because he shrugged out of his tux jacket and tossed it aside without breaking contact with Archie's mouth. He then peeled off Archie's jacket, tie, and vest. Probably everything would get discarded on the floor and end up terribly wrinkled, but Archie wasn't sure he cared.

He wanted to see more of Ondrej, so he started unwrapping him, reverently taking off each piece of clothing, wanting to savor the moment. He tried to aim discarded clothing at a chair or the dresser to save it from a horrible fate on the floor, but he wasn't sure he made it that often. He was too focused on kissing

Ondrej, running his hands through Ondrej's hair, tasting Ondrej's lips, pressing his hips against Ondrej's.

Ondrej reached between them and slid his fingers under Archie's belt loops. "Yes," Archie mumbled, unable to make coherent sentences. Ondrej undid the belt at a leisurely pace, pulling the leather through the loop, and then he very slowly undid the zipper, grazing his fingers over Archie's cock. Archie was hard and straining against his briefs, and Ondrej must have felt that. Ondrej rubbed his fingers gently over the bulge he was revealing before he stepped back and slid Archie's pants over his hips. When the belt hit the floor, Archie stepped out of his pants.

"You're less elegant out of your clothes," Ondrej commented, undoing his own belt. "Less fancy. Less wealthy. Just a man."

"I'm always just a man," Archie said.

"No. I think sometimes you're more than that."

Archie couldn't ask what Ondrej meant by that because Ondrej kissed him again as he wriggled out of his pants. Then they both stood there in their underwear, facing each other. Ondrej lifted an eyebrow. Archie gestured toward the bed. Ondrej grinned and stepped backward. He danced a bit as he pulled off his socks, and then he flopped onto the bed on his back, his hard cock pushing against the front of his briefs. Feeling no more nerves, Archie shucked his own briefs and climbed onto the bed.

Ondrej grinned again and put his arms around Archie. They kissed again, and Archie took the opportunity to run his hands down the front of Ondrej's naked chest. Ondrej was in surprisingly good shape for someone who spent as much time lounging on the sofa in the den as he did. His pecs were clearly defined, he had a flat stomach, and round muscles bulged on his arms as he moved them. Archie liked the contrast in their bodies too, the way he was a little bigger than Ondrej and could cover him, protect him, maybe. It made him feel possessive, like he had something in his arms now worth cherishing. Perhaps he did.

Ondrej shifted his weight on the bed and spread his legs. Oh, that was more like it. Archie moved between Ondrej's legs until his bare cock lined up with Ondrej's still-clothed one. That touch alone sent sparks through Archie's body. He dipped his head and kissed Ondrej as he thrust against him. His pulse raced and he felt hot everywhere as he hooked his fingers into the waistband of Ondrej's briefs and gave them a tug.

"Naked," he murmured.

Ondrej laughed softly. He nudged Archie away and took off his briefs, exposing himself completely to Archie for the first time. His cock was hard and large, his whole body defying expectation. He was tan and sexy, and he cocked an eyebrow at Archie in an inviting way.

So Archie took Ondrej's cock and stroked it. Ondrej arched off the bed and moaned. Archie kissed that moan off his lips, causing Ondrej to writhe beneath him. Yes, *yes*, this was what Archie wanted. He wanted Ondrej to surrender to the pleasure they could make together. Archie shifted closer and pressed his cock into Ondrej's hip, thrusting against him, getting off a little.

Lord, it had been a long time since he'd been with anyone. Fuzzy nervousness and arousal and relief flooded his veins. They were moving toward something, Archie knew it, and it wasn't just a hot fuck. Realizing that made Archie's pulse race even more. He backed off slightly because he was suddenly worried about coming too soon. But this was so good and Ondrej was so hot, and now he was touching Archie, running his hands over Archie's chest and pinching his nipples. Archie groaned and moved closer again, wanting to press the whole length of his body against Ondrej's.

They kissed more, and Ondrej maneuvered Archie until he was on top, his hips nestled between Ondrej's parted legs again, only this time they were both naked. They were hot and slick, from sweat now, mostly, and they moved against each other as if they'd been doing this for years.

Archie wanted to be inside Ondrej but was afraid to suggest it. Maybe that was too much too fast.

But then Ondrej said, "I want you inside me."

Archie groaned in answer, unable to say what he was feeling, which was that he'd be happy to fuck Ondrej until dawn and he knew it would be perfect.

He pulled lube from his nightstand.

"That was fast," Ondrej said.

"I want you," Archie said into Ondrej's skin. "I've been wanting you for weeks."

Ondrej sighed and leaned back a little. So Archie took the lube and poured a generous amount on his fingers. He slipped his fingers over Ondrej's hole, which caused Ondrej to groan.

"Not a virgin, then," Ondrej whispered shakily.

"No. I didn't think either of us were."

"Me neither, but I wasn't sure. We haven't talked about it."

"Must we now?" He thrust a finger inside Ondrej.

Ondrej cough-laughed and arched off the bed again. "Just...." He pressed a hand to Archie's chest. "I saw the doctor a month ago. I don't have anything. We're married. I...."

Archie closed his eyes. "We're committed." What Archie meant was that they were in a relationship in which neither of them would sleep with anybody else. Archie hadn't had sex in so long that there was no way he could have contracted anything. He let out a breath. "I would never do anything to put you in danger."

Ondrej closed his eyes and nodded. "I know."

The trust meant a lot coming from Ondrej. "Should I stop so we can have a longer discussion?" He was teasing, and to show it, he pressed another finger into Ondrej and curled it, hoping to hit his prostate.

"Absolutely not." Ondrej arched off the bed again. "Oh God. Do that again."

Ondrej grabbed Archie's arms and dug his fingernails into Archie's skin as Archie prepared him. He writhed again, clearly enjoying it, throwing his head back and moaning. Then he said, "God, Archie, if you don't fuck me right now, I'll lose my goddamn mind."

"Can't have that," Archie said, stroking himself and then tossing the lube aside. He lined himself up at Ondrej's hole and pressed forward slightly. "Is this okay?"

"Yes, God, more!"

So Archie thrust forward. Again, he was conscious of the fact that he was bigger than Ondrej, that Ondrej was vulnerable and beneath him. It felt like an awesome responsibility to take care of him. Ondrej threw his head back against the pillow and shouted, "More!" It pulled Archie into the moment, and he started to thrust.

Ondrej was tight and hot, and it felt amazing to be inside him bare. Archie thrust, building up momentum, loving the friction and the way Ondrej's body squeezed him. It was raw, sweating and grunting, something animalistic, but it was beautiful too, because they were kissing and touching and expressing whatever had changed between them as they'd danced with each other that night. Maybe they weren't in love, but they had something new, something worth holding on to.

Archie had the fleeting thought that they were officially consummating their marriage. It was a step over the threshold; there was no going back now.

Then the thought drifted away as Archie's brain shorted out and he could only feel. His body tingled, and he felt suddenly as if he were running toward a cliff. He took a deep breath and slowed down, hoping to drag this out before he jumped into oblivion, but then Ondrej said, "God, faster, harder. I'm almost there."

So Archie let loose, no longer holding himself back. He thrust hard and fast into Ondrej and reached between them to stroke Ondrej's cock. He made magic, and the orgasm built somewhere near the base of Archie's spine. He held his breath, not willing to give in to it yet but not willing to let up on Ondrej, who clawed at Archie's shoulders and let loose a string of moaned profanity, or so Archie assumed, since not all of the words were English.

Then Ondrej murmured Archie's name and thrust against him and came, clamping down on Archie's cock and pumping against his hand. Ondrej spurted against both of their chests, moaning the whole time, his cock vibrating in Archie's hand. It was ecstatic and beautiful.

Archie couldn't hold back anymore.

He let go of Ondrej's cock and grabbed his hips, holding on for dear life as he kept thrusting at just the pace he needed to get there. Once he felt the inevitable tingle in his balls, he grasped Ondrej's shoulders and pulled him into his arms. He held Ondrej close as he pumped his hips one more time and spilled inside him, coming on a groan.

It wasn't until he began to come back down from his orgasm that he felt Ondrej's arms around him too. Then Ondrej pressed kisses all over Archie's face. Archie had the presence of mind to shift his chin so that he could kiss Ondrej straight on the lips. Ondrej groaned into his mouth.

"God, that was good," Ondrej whispered.

Archie laughed despite himself. He was getting soft, but he was reluctant to pull out of Ondrej just yet. Alas, nature took over, and Archie had to back away when he started to get itchy.

"It was good," he said.

"You know," Ondrej said, "if in, like, half an hour, you wanted to do that again, I'd be game."

"You could also spend the whole weekend here with me, in this bed."

"I could."

"I'd make it worth your while."

Ondrej smirked. "I bet you would."

"Seriously, though. Just as soon as I can get it up again, I want you."

Ondrej sat up a little. "Yeah, me too. Crazy, huh?"

Archie lay back down beside Ondrej. "I mean, I have no plans this weekend. I was serious about spending the whole time in bed together."

Ondrej rolled over and draped an arm over Archie. "I have no problem with that plan."

Archie kissed him soundly. "Good. So no rush, then. If I wanted to take a quick nap or get a snack, you wouldn't object?"

"I didn't eat enough at the party, either. Too much pretentious finger food, not enough real food."

Archie smiled and hugged Ondrej to him. "I could really go for a steak right now."

Ondrej laughed. "Oh God, me too. Do you think there's anywhere that will still deliver one at this time of night?"

"It's New York City. Of course there is. The twenty-four-hour diner on Amsterdam makes a decent steak."

Ondrej pulled away from Archie and scrambled out of bed. "Where's my phone? Let's make this happen."

Archie laughed and got out of bed.

Chapter Nine

ONDREJ puttered around the house, bored. Archie had invited him to come along to the office, but he'd declined. He wanted to live another day in the delusion that things would work out, thus kicking the stadium-discussion can further down the road. Ondrej was becoming increasingly convinced that continued investment in a new stadium would bankrupt the already fragile Katsaros Holdings, which reiterated his general feeling that investing in Katsaros was like throwing money down a trash chute. But things with Archie were going so well that he didn't want to face that just yet.

Nothing in the house was terribly interesting, though. He'd already pored over every inch of it during his first few days as a resident. Going by his house alone, Archie seemed tremendously boring. Oh, he kept books everywhere, and a video game console sat next to the TV in the den, and a couple of raunchy gay porn videos were tucked away in a hidden corner of the armoire where he kept DVDs. But Archie was not really one for secrets. He clearly kept his financial documents mostly in the office downtown, because his home office was cluttered with knickknacks but otherwise held little of interest. Hildy kept most of the common areas in pristine condition; the rooms were largely ornamental and not practical. Ondrej assumed Archie maintained the rooms in deference to his late mother. The only rooms that seemed lived-in were the den, where Ondrej spent most of his time these days, and Archie's bedroom, where Ondrej had just spent the last few nights... and would perhaps spend more nights in the future.

But that remained to be seen. The bubble seemed to have burst when Archie left for work that morning.

Ondrej plopped down on the sofa, figuring he could at least numb his brain with daytime TV. Then the house phone rang.

After Ondrej answered it, a woman said, "I'm Nancy Smalls. I'm calling from US Citizenship and Immigration Services? I have a green card application from an Ondrej Kovac?"

"Speaking." Ondrej was impressed Ms. Smalls had gotten his name right on the first try—though she probably dealt with non-English names daily—but butterflies still swirled through his chest. Here was where he'd get caught. Everyone he'd talked to had sworn green cards were fairly easy to obtain and CIS rarely investigated. So why were they calling?

"Yes, hi, Mr. Kovac. It says here you've applied for a change in visa status. You're aware your work visa expired three weeks ago."

"Yes. But I got married, so I applied for the change." He took a deep breath. This would get worse if the clerk on the other end was homophobic, but he figured he might as well put it all out there. "My husband is a US citizen."

"Yes. Of course. Well, I'd like to schedule an interview. Just to check on things. See how you're adjusting. And, of course, I have to verify a few things in order to process the paperwork. When will you and your husband be available next week?"

Ondrej still didn't know Archie's schedule very well, but he reasoned that, as owner of his company, Archie could take off whenever he wanted to, unless he had a board meeting scheduled. And since he was pretending to be a kept man, Ondrej's schedule was wide open. He negotiated an appointment for later in the week.

After he hung up the phone, he stared at the blank screen of the TV. Now he fretted about Nancy Smalls on top of being bored. He'd spent the better part of the summer exploring the city, but he could go to museums by himself only so many times, and now that he was married to Archie and had gotten his photo published in the tabloids and on Priscilla Zimmer's website, it wasn't like he could kill time by flirting with boys at bars—not that he wanted to do that, either, not after the weekend with Archie. He felt trapped, purposeless. He knew Archie had offered him an opportunity with that office at Katsaros Holdings, and he intended to use it, but… if he'd wanted to spend all day in an office, he could have stayed in Prague.

But he couldn't stop thinking about what things Nancy Smalls had to verify. He wondered how wide the perception that he'd married Archie for his money was. He must have looked like a real asshole to anyone who assumed Ondrej had married Archie both for the money and the green card. How easy would it be for CIS to look into Archie's finances and see that he was broke? Would they see the money Ondrej had invested as the payment it really was? Would they buy that Archie and Ondrej were really in love? What would happen if they denied Ondrej's application?

He had to do something to distract himself from the questions swirling in his mind. But what the hell was he going to do with himself?

He thought about calling Archie to tell him about the interview, but he figured the best way to alleviate his boredom would be to get out of the house.

ARCHIE was surprised to see Ondrej at the door of his office.

"I thought you were staying home today."

Ondrej stepped inside and closed the door. "I was, but we have a problem."

"Is this about the stadium project? Because—"

Ondrej shook his head vigorously and sat down in one of the spare chairs. He still wanted to discuss that, but other issues were more pressing. "I got a call from immigration. Well, Citizenship and Immigration Services."

"Oh." Archie broke out in a cold sweat. Despite everything, he still felt the hovering threat that this fraud was about to be exposed. Maybe he and Ondrej were forging their way toward something, but they certainly weren't madly in love. Things with Ondrej felt fragile, still.

"The agent who called wanted to set up an interview." Ondrej shook his head again. "I read online that most green cards applied for because of marriage are approved because CIS doesn't have the resources to interview or investigate, so I really thought we were in the clear as long as we kept up the act in public."

Archie had thought the same thing. He'd had Marketa investigate when they'd first cooked up this plan, and she'd essentially told him they'd be fine.

"I assume," said Ondrej, "that timing plays a role. The agent who called seemed suspicious of the fact that my work visa expired right before we got married. And this case was probably also brought to her attention because of your relatively high profile."

Archie frowned. Of course. His name had been bandied about in the news since before his father had died. He'd been dubbed one of New York's most eligible bachelors when he'd been in his twenties. He'd tried to avoid media attention, but it still found him sometimes. Most people who reported on business assumed he'd take the helm of the company, and now he was involved in this new Eagles stadium project in Brooklyn, so he supposed hiding from reporters wasn't an option. He still thought the stadium was a good investment, especially if the Eagles continued to play baseball well and get people in the stadium for home games. His plans included ways to easily convert the space to a concert venue and multiuse space in the off-season. The retractable dome in the original plan would likely have to be scrapped, but a streamlined approach to building this stadium could potentially save the company. It was a good long-term plan, Archie maintained. Hopefully Ondrej's money and a few solid investors would keep them afloat in the meantime.

But it was risky. The last project on this scale in the city had lost its developers quite a bit of money in the short term. They had made it back quickly once the venue opened, but it was the sort of hit that Katsaros might not be able to recover from. Archie thought they could still pull it off if they were smart about it. Convincing Ondrej and the board of the efficacy of this plan would be tricky.

But that was neither here nor there if Ondrej was deported.

"The interview is next Thursday afternoon. She requested your presence as well."

"All right." Archie mentally ran through his calendar. "That should be okay."

"We should probably… I don't know. Practice. She might ask some probing questions, and there's still a lot we don't know about each other."

It was taking a lot to stem the tide of Archie's panic. There was no way they'd be able to pull this off convincingly. Ondrej was right; despite the sex-fueled weekend, they still barely knew each other. Archie only really knew the surface; he knew where all of Ondrej's scars and moles and imperfections were. He'd spent hours looking at and touching all of Ondrej's skin. He was more enchanted with the man now than he had been a week ago. But all he really knew about the man inside the body was that Ondrej had grown up in Prague and seemed to have a good sense of business. He had a sardonic sense of humor. But… did he have brothers and sisters? Did he have childhood pets? What was he doing in Prague before he moved to the States? What did his parents do? Archie didn't know.

"Are you… are you panicking?" Ondrej asked.

Archie hadn't realized his breath had gotten short. He was suddenly having trouble pulling in air. "I… I think maybe…."

It wasn't quite a panic attack. Archie knew what those felt like, despite not having had one in years. But it was a prelude to something more serious if he couldn't get his breathing under control. He tried to take in a deep breath, but it was shaky.

Ondrej ran around the desk in a flash, placing a hand on the back of Archie's neck. "Bend forward. Put your head between your legs. Deep breaths."

Archie did as he was told and managed to at least get his breathing back to normal, but the panic didn't subside much. "What the hell are we going to do?" he asked from between his legs.

"Not sure." Ondrej rubbed Archie's back. It felt like affection. "But we could try to get to know each other. Spend time together. We've got about a week and a half to figure it out."

Archie sat back up and looked at Ondrej. "All right. I suppose I'm game if you are. Maybe we can find something interesting to do together this weekend."

It felt a little like asking his own husband out on a date, but Ondrej smiled and said, "That sounds lovely."

"Did you really come down here just to tell me we were going to be interviewed by a woman from CIS?"

"Mostly, yes. I was feeling restless at home."

"Do you plan to stick around this afternoon?"

"I just might. Shall we get dinner together later?"

And that felt a little like being asked on a date too. That was likely not Ondrej's intention, but something about his tone made Archie think Ondrej really did want them to get to know each other better, perhaps for a goal beyond just impressing a woman from immigration services. "I'd like that," Archie said.

Ondrej grinned. "Good. Then I'll abuse your hospitality by getting some coffee and reading in my office. Do you want anything from the kitchen?"

"No, I'm all right." And that felt like the truth.

Chapter Ten

AN opportunity to carry through with the "spend time together" plan presented itself later that week. Cathleen Brandt sent Archie an e-mail about some sort of yachting event, saying Archie really should put in an appearance if he was to live up to his reputation as the gay Aristotle Onassis.

"Yachts?" Ondrej said when Archie mentioned the invitation.

"Big fancy boats."

Ondrej sighed and sank into his chair at the kitchen table. "I know what a yacht is. It's just… considering we're trying to bail out your company, it just seems like such a conspicuous show of wealth."

"I realize that. But we want a conspicuous show of wealth. We want people to think Katsaros is succeeding." Archie pulled out his phone and pulled up the e-mail to show Ondrej. "The thing is, nobody knows the current state of the company, so you and I being conspicuous would probably be good for us. If the usual set is there, probably there will be press. That would make us look good, yes? And it's probably good for business if I seem confident and not like a failure."

Ondrej sighed as Archie handed him the phone. He read the e-mail and passed the phone back. "I suppose you're right."

"Not to mention, us being seen publicly together might impress Ms. Smalls."

"That is true."

"My cousin has a nice boat at a marina near Bridgeport, Connecticut, that she'd likely let us borrow for an afternoon."

"Can you drive it?"

Archie raised an eyebrow. "I grew up with a Greek man who loved the sea. I was raised in boats like this. I could drive it in my sleep. But it's hardly racing. We drive leisurely around the sound for a couple of hours and then go to a party at a yacht club near the marina."

"Just us on the boat?"

"If that's what you want. We can invite people to come along. My cousin loves these kinds of things. Her name is Samantha, goes by Sam. She's my mother's sister's daughter. Most of my other friends have their own boats, but if you wanted to bring Amy, that would be all right." Amy seemed to be the person in New York Ondrej was closest to.

"All right. I'll think on it."

Archie pocketed his phone and said, "It could be fun. The sun, the sea air. We'd be on a boat that cost more than some apartments. Sam spared no expense.

It's a gorgeous boat with lots of amenities. Then we'll go to the party and I'll show you off."

Ondrej shot Archie a rueful smile, but then he laughed. "Will there be liquor at this party?"

"Undoubtedly. Probably pretentious finger food too."

"Oh, well, if pretentious food is involved."

Archie grinned despite himself. He leaned over and gave Ondrej a quick peck on the cheek. "I will admit to an ulterior motive, in that I think a few of the executives at potential corporate sponsors for the stadium project might be at the party, and I'd like to get a little schmoozy."

Ondrej nodded slowly. "Yes. I understand why it's important."

"So you'll go?"

"Yes, all right. But I'm bringing Amy. And Dramamine. I'm not great on boats."

"Deal."

"**THIS** is amazing," Amy said.

Ondrej begged to differ. It was probably only a matter of time before he lost his lunch over the side of this damn huge boat. He sat on the top deck with Amy, who insisted the air in his face would help with the seasickness, but Ondrej was pretty sure his nausea wouldn't ease until he got back on solid land.

Samantha and her husband, Todd, sat across from Ondrej and Amy. Todd seemed very stiff, but Sam kept enthusiastically pointing out landmarks and interesting things on the shoreline. Ondrej didn't look; he found if he focused on a particular point on the horizon, the nausea wasn't unbearable. But Amy seemed to be eating it up.

Archie stood before the steering wheel, sunglasses shading his eyes, and he looked like he belonged there. He was remarkably handsome, his curly hair falling rakishly over his forehead, his clothes expensive and well tailored, the goatee making him look a little disreputable. His confidence behind the wheel was dead sexy.

Ondrej just wished he didn't feel so ill, so he could better appreciate his handsome husband.

"I've never been on a boat this nice," Amy said, mostly to Sam. "My parents have a little speedboat they take out on a lake in Connecticut, and it's nice, but this makes it look like a cardboard box. Lord. Feel how soft these seats are, Ondrej. Like butter." She stroked the seats.

"If you guys get hungry, I packed sandwich fixings and chips and things in the kitchen downstairs." Sam gestured toward the little ladder that led below deck.

At the prospect of food, Ondrej nearly lost it again. He clutched his stomach and hung on to the railing.

"You look green," Amy said.

"I'll be okay once the Dramamine kicks in."

"What you need is a distraction. Hey, Archie!"

Archie fiddled with the speed of the boat. They weren't even going very fast, but apparently it was just fast enough for Ondrej's body to realize they were on the water. They slowed down more and Archie said, "What?"

"Come tend to your husband."

Archie glanced back at them. "Ondrej? Are you all right?"

"I think I'm dying."

Todd hopped up. "I can take over driving."

So Archie handed over the wheel and walked over to sit next to Ondrej. "You really aren't good on boats."

"I come from a landlocked country. What do you want from me?"

"Isn't there a river in Prague?" Amy asked.

"Shut up."

Archie held out a hand. "Come with me to the kitchen. We'll see if we can find some ginger ale."

"Okay." Ondrej took Archie's hand.

Ondrej was surprised to learn that once they were below deck and the shoreline wasn't zipping by, he didn't feel quite so sick. Archie led him into the kitchen, which was tiny but still very nice. Archie opened a little fridge and pulled out a small bottle of ginger ale and handed it to Ondrej.

Ondrej took a few slow breaths. When he struggled to get the bottle open, Archie stepped forward and opened it for him, and their fingers brushed. It was such a sweet little gesture, it made Ondrej's heart ache.

"Thank you," Ondrej said.

"Is it really that bad?"

Ondrej took a few sips of ginger ale and tried to gauge how he felt. "It's a little better."

Archie grinned. "Am I helping?"

Ondrej couldn't help but smile back. "A little."

Archie smoothed an errant lock of hair off of Ondrej's face. He leaned forward and kissed Ondrej's forehead. Near the comforting warmth of Archie's body, Ondrej forgot all about the rocking sea for a moment.

He wanted to hug Archie, to get closer to that comfort, so he did. He wrapped an arm around Archie's torso, and Archie returned the hug. It was... nice. Ondrej had slept around a bit when he first got to New York, but he hadn't realized how starved he was for genuine affection until he moved into Archie's house. And for the past week, he'd had it in abundance.

"Are you finding everything all right?" Sam called out. She walked into the kitchen and laughed. "Sorry, didn't mean to interrupt."

"It's fine," said Archie, peeling himself away.

Ondrej missed his touch but settled for sipping his ginger ale.

"Newlyweds," Sam said, giggling. "I remember what that was like."

"It's not romantic if I vomit all over Archie."

"Give Todd a little time to show off at the wheel. Then we can head back to shore."

Ondrej nodded. He hated to cut this little cruise short, but he was miserable. He sipped more ginger ale and rubbed his forehead. "Sorry. I'm not cut out for boats."

"Happens to the best of us." Sam smiled and patted Archie's shoulder. "You'll note my daughter is not here. She also never got her sea legs. Pukes every time we're out on the water."

Archie laughed. He threw his arm around Ondrej and started to steer him back toward the ladder up to the deck. "And how is Desiree?"

"Just fine. High school interviews now. Dalton seems promising."

They chatted about school and teenage girl things as Ondrej settled back into his seat on the deck. He was somewhat less nauseated, and drinking ginger ale gave him an excuse not to contribute to the conversation. Amy gave him a sympathetic look and a pat on the knee.

If this didn't get better, it would be a long day.

ONDREJ still looked quite pale as they headed into the yacht club. Archie held out his arm, and Ondrej slipped his hand through it and then wrapped his arms around it.

"Still feeling woozy?"

Ondrej answered by pressing his face into Archie's shoulder.

Sam clucked her tongue as if she disapproved, but Amy laughed, apparently enjoying Ondrej's distress.

Cathleen Brandt greeted Archie amiably and asked after Ondrej.

"We went out on Sam's boat today," Archie said. "Ondrej doesn't quite have his sea legs yet."

"Not a boat," Ondrej said into Archie's arm. "Nausea-inducing machine."

Cathleen laughed. "That gets better, darling. I got sick the first time I went out on the *Celtic Mermaid*."

"That's the name of the Brandt yacht," Archie said to Ondrej.

He picked up his head and smiled weakly at Cathleen. "I gathered."

"My family has been driving boats around Long Island Sound for generations, so my father kept insisting it would come naturally to me. It's better than it used to be, but I still get a little seasick sometimes."

Ondrej nodded.

"Archie, you still love the sea, yeah?"

Archie reached over to smooth some of Ondrej's hair off his sweaty brow. "Yes. Always have. I hadn't actually been on the sound in a while, though."

Ondrej sighed. "I'm sorry for making us turn back early."

"It's fine. I got to drive around for a bit. I'm sure I will again soon."

"Well, there's food everywhere." Cathleen gestured around the room. "Maybe you're not ready to partake just yet, but the little quiche things the waiters are walking around with are particularly divine."

Cathleen moved on to greet other guests. Archie worried about Ondrej feeling so miserable, but then Ondrej pointed out there was a bar. "I think something fizzy would do the trick."

So Archie got him a drink and then took him around to meet various party guests.

An older woman Archie didn't know approached and air-kissed Sam. "Lovely to see you, Samantha."

"You know my cousin, Archie Katsaros," Sam said.

Archie shook hands with the woman.

"Oh, of course. The gay Aristotle Onassis. That's what the society pages are calling you, isn't it?"

Archie was starting to hate that nickname. He glanced at Sam but said, "I suppose so."

"Archie, this is Phyllis Decker. She—"

Phyllis reached out her hand. "Of the Westport Deckers."

"Of course," Archie said, the name only vaguely familiar.

"And the barnacle attached to your arm is your new spouse, I suppose."

Ondrej picked his head up again and extended the hand that wasn't tucked into Archie's upper arm. "Charmed," he said.

"Ondrej's still a little seasick," Archie said. "Anyway, the Onassis comparison is one I've heard before, but I'm not sure it's really apt."

"Both Greek tycoons, no?"

Archie couldn't help but frown. "I suppose."

"He told me to start shopping for pillbox hats," Ondrej said quietly. "He enjoys the comparison. I suppose if I ever learn to ride in a boat, I could wear big Jackie O sunglasses."

"What you need," Phyllis said, holding up one hand, "is a project. Something to invest in. I know you're young, but this is where you make or break your career."

Archie didn't want business advice from a woman who looked old enough to be his grandmother. He wondered at her credentials. Maybe he was being shortsighted, but he couldn't imagine how someone as old and blue-blooded as Phyllis could know what Archie should be doing with his time.

"Phyllis owns a majority share in Olympic Shipping," Sam said.

And then it all fell into place. Olympic Shipping was one of the largest freight carriers in the country. They controlled the distribution of goods by train and plane throughout a good chunk of the United States. And she owned a majority share? Archie felt guilty for misjudging her.

To Ondrej, Phyllis said, "I inherited the position of CEO from my late husband, but I took to being executive like a fish to water."

"It's true," said Sam.

Archie nodded, because he recalled now that Phyllis had been tremendously successful, modernizing the company and expanding its portfolio. She could be an ally after all. "Perhaps a longer conversation is in order at a later date," Archie said. "As the new chair of Katsaros Holdings, I'm looking to take the company into the twenty-first century and beyond."

It was a corny line, but it did the trick. "Investments, my dear boy, and smart ones are what you need. What do you have in mind?"

"A new baseball stadium."

She nodded. "Yes, of course. A fine project, one that could be quite lucrative. I would like to discuss it with you further when I have not had so much champagne. Shall we do lunch next week?"

After Archie and Phyllis exchanged information, Ondrej finally let go of Archie's arm.

"Feel better?" Archie asked.

"Yes, and I'm amazed you handled that as smoothly as you did. Well done."

"I'm not terrible at this schmoozing thing."

"No. Not at all."

"Katsaros is investing in the Eagles stadium project?" asked Todd, coming alive suddenly.

Amy seemed interested too. "I hadn't heard that, either."

"If Archie has his way," said Ondrej.

"If I prove to the board it's a sound investment," said Archie. "I think it is."

Todd babbled about baseball for a few minutes. Archie had trouble following as Todd delved into his deep knowledge of players and statistics—Archie was really more of a casual fan—but he nodded and smiled and murmured affirmative-sounding monosyllables when it seemed appropriate.

"So you're in favor," Archie concluded.

"Oh, absolutely. Maybe we should have lunch too."

Archie was thus feeling pretty good an hour later, after he'd discussed his investment plans with a dozen other people. Quite a few people had indicated they were willing to sign on, which made Archie feel like he could raise the seed money he needed to get the project off the ground.

"I'm impressed," Ondrej said, sipping white wine now that his stomach had finally settled. "You may just pull this off."

"It's only promises of meetings and further discussion. It's nothing concrete yet."

"No, but I don't think I've ever seen you in action this way before. It's kind of sexy."

"Yeah?"

"Yeah. Look at you, wheeling and dealing. I like this business Archie much more than the one who yells at his employees."

"A kinder, gentler approach, yeah?"

"Exactly." Ondrej smiled. "Is there anyone else here I just *have* to meet?"

"Not really. We can head back to the city after you finish your wine, if you like."

"Will there be dancing, do you think?"

There was soft music playing, but Archie had seen a group of guys carry instrument cases in a few minutes before. "Probably."

"Then let's stay for one dance."

"You want to dance with me?"

"Of course. I enjoy dancing with you. All that blue blood, I suppose." Ondrej smiled. "You've got proper dancing bred into you."

Archie smiled, touched that Ondrej would want to display their newfound affection for each other so publicly. "I'd love to dance, then. We can stay for as many dances as you like."

Ondrej smiled, and he looked so boyish and handsome as he did so that Archie was charmed. He reached over and took Ondrej's hand, threaded their fingers together.

Sam strolled by and made gagging noises. "You lovebirds are the worst. Young love, who needs it?"

Archie laughed. "Thanks, Sam."

Sam grinned. "I'm not going to lie, there's something of a pool going about whether your marriage is legit. Someone caught wind of the fact that Ondrej, here, applied for a green card."

"To stay with Archie," Ondrej said.

"Well, *I* know that. I'm looking forward to telling all the stuffed shirts at the yacht club about how you two are so sickeningly adorable."

"Thanks," said Archie. "I think."

Sam playfully punched Archie in the arm. "Ondrej's seasickness notwithstanding, you seem really happy. Are you happy, Archie?"

Archie looked at Ondrej. "You know? I think I might just be."

Chapter Eleven

ON Monday, after the weekend haze had worn off, Archie spent some time on his Eagles stadium proposal for the board. He stepped out of his office to ask Marketa what it would cost to put together a glossy booklet that was sure to impress any potential investor. Ondrej arrived at her desk at the same time Archie did.

"Hello," Archie greeted him. For show, he leaned over and gave Ondrej a quick peck on the lips. Or perhaps that was for himself; Marketa knew exactly what kind of marriage Archie and Ondrej had.

"Hello, Archie." Ondrej smiled. "I realized I left a book in my office last week, so I came by to fetch it. Are you busy?"

"Unfortunately."

"Maybe I'll do some work, then."

Ondrej walked down the hall to his office. Archie watched him go before turning back to Marketa and asking his question. After she agreed to look into it, he went back to his office and the stadium proposal. He was distracted now, however, preoccupied with the idea of Ondrej working just down the hall.

The yacht club party had been stuffy but kind of fun, in retrospect. It wasn't as formal as a charity gala. Archie had felt more in his element. Archie's acquaintances seemed to be getting used to Ondrej and Archie as a couple. Dancing with Ondrej had been fun and romantic. They'd come home from the party and spent most of Sunday in bed, lounging and talking and eating whatever they could get delivered. It had been nice. More fun than Archie'd had in months.

Monday morning was like a step back into reality. He knew Ondrej still had some reservations about the stadium project, but they hadn't discussed it. Instead, they'd made some unspoken arrangement not to bring it up, perhaps to maintain harmony. Or because there was a more pressing problem: they still had to contend with the prospect of the woman from immigration interviewing them later in the week. Thinking about that made Archie feel panicky again.

Later in the afternoon, Ondrej dropped by. "So I've been thinking about this interview Thursday."

Archie let out a breath. "You too? I've been obsessing over it all afternoon instead of working."

Ondrej nodded. "Well, I was thinking. Are you free for dinner tonight? We could go on an actual date."

"A date?"

"That's when two people go out together and try to get to know each other."

"Yes, I know what a date is. You want to go on a date with me?"

Ondrej smiled. "You are my husband."

Archie kept forgetting that. "Right. Well, okay."

"We can compare notes. Make sure we each know enough about each other to fool the interviewer."

Of course. A practical date, not a romantic date. Because sex and the last couple of weeks aside, some of their interactions still felt like business transactions. "All right. I can do dinner."

"Good. All right. Back to work, then. Perhaps not today, but at some point in the near future, I would like to go over some of the operating expenses, see where we can trim some fat. And we should talk about this stadium project. You seem determined to go forward with it."

Archie's stomach dropped. So much for harmony. "It's a good investment."

"It's a financial sinkhole. Was the project yours or your father's idea?"

"My father's." Which Archie supposed absolved him of some of the insanity behind the project. But the stadium was the first project under the Katsaros umbrella that had actually sparked something in Archie. He felt enthusiasm for it that he hadn't felt for any of his other projects. Katsaros Holdings owned a half-dozen apartment buildings around the city, a mix of new construction and old buildings that had been renovated to eradicate all uniqueness, and Archie was strongly considering selling a few to make up for the financial deficits, but Marketa kept telling him that would be bad business. And he knew that. The competitive real estate market meant that the vacancy rate in Katsaros buildings was close to nothing, so those buildings were a sure source of income, provided no major repairs had to be made. The stadium was a bigger question mark. It was a risk. Which somehow made it more appealing to Archie.

Maybe he had something of his father in him after all.

"Did you get the information from your managers about staff performance?" Ondrej asked.

"Yes. Marketa has a file."

"I'll start there, then. I'll have recommendations by the Friday board meeting."

"All right."

Ondrej walked out of the office, leaving Archie feeling uneasy. He could recognize that the company was spinning out of his control, but he didn't like handing over so much of it to a relative stranger. He trusted Ondrej, but surrendering part of the company felt a little like giving up part of his soul.

Chapter Twelve

ONDREJ met Archie at his office at the appointed time. "I took the liberty of making a reservation at Vin et Fromage," he said.

"Great," said Archie, grabbing his briefcase.

They walked in relative silence from the office to the restaurant. Ondrej was still turning over questions in his head. He'd divided his time that afternoon between going over personnel files and researching questions he might be asked in his immigration interview. He'd made a list, which he'd uploaded to his phone so he could take notes. Which made this feel more like an academic exercise than a date, but maybe that was for the best. After a long weekend of sex that Ondrej had thoroughly enjoyed, he worried about getting too emotionally attached to Archie to be rational about the task at hand.

Although… they were married, for goodness' sake. Did Ondrej really intend to leave Archie in a year? Was there really any harm in an emotional attachment? Ondrej had been resisting it from the outset, but maybe he didn't have to. He'd just assumed that, once he had his green card in hand, he'd move on, but if nothing else, the last couple of weeks had shown him he had a spark with Archie. So why did he shy away from it?

For one thing, the line between reality and fraud was blurring in a way Ondrej found disquieting. Not to mention all the money at stake. Ondrej had to work out the financial details before any of this had a hope of being viable. He worried Archie was further in debt than he was saying. It was one thing not to have enough information to adequately assess the situation. It was quite another for Archie to be less than honest.

Once they were seated at the restaurant, Archie picked up a menu and said, "Did you discover any dead weight in your examination of my employees' files?"

"Possibly. I'll be able to tell better by the board meeting."

Archie nodded and focused his attention on the menu.

After they'd ordered, Ondrej got out his phone. "Before you think I'm unforgivably rude, I wrote down some questions."

Archie pursed his lips. "I suppose it was too much to ask for this date to be like a real date where things develop organically."

"These are strange circumstances."

"I'll say."

But Ondrej took a deep breath and began.

They covered a lot of basics. Ondrej was an only child. Both of his parents were alive and well in Prague. His father was distant and his mother was overbearing.

Archie also had no siblings, but he had grown up with a few cousins on his mother's side and was godfather to one cousin's son. Archie had gone to private schools in the city, and then Columbia undergrad and NYU Stern for his MBA. Ondrej had dropped out of Charles University in Prague, had gone to work for his grandparents' vineyard in France, and then spent a couple of years living it up in Prague while working for his parents before deciding he needed a change of scenery and leaving for New York.

"But you must have done well for yourself," Archie pointed out.

"My money is mostly inherited," Ondrej said. "It's my grandparents' money. They left Czechoslovakia when I was young to escape the oppressive regime there. My mother stayed behind to marry my father."

"How did you learn business, then?"

"I suppose I mostly picked it up by listening to my grandparents talk. Grandma in particular was a shrewd businesswoman. It's why she left Prague. The government was actively putting down any kind of creativity and thought the economy would thrive if everyone stuck to tried-and-true methods. There were a lot of regulations about how you could run a business. It was actually confining and probably did more damage than good." Ondrej smiled. "There's your history lesson for the day."

Archie nodded. "I'll admit, I know very little about Czech history."

"There's a lot of it. I was a kid at the end of the Cold War, so I don't remember much about the worst of it, but my parents tell stories." Ondrej sipped his water. "I worked for my parents when I lived in Prague, but we don't get along very well, so that wasn't a workable situation. And before you ask, I think it's just normal parent-son nonsense. They had specific ideas about who I should be, and I never quite met their expectations."

Archie nodded, so presumably he understood that, or at least knew not to probe. He'd seen Ondrej's breakdown after informing his mother about his marriage, so he probably knew enough about how troubled that relationship was. Archie said instead, "All right. How did you learn English?"

"School. Private tutors. I watched a lot of American movies, as well."

Archie smiled. "I have always been struck by how your accent is more American than British. I just assumed Europeans learned British English."

"Some do, I suppose." Ondrej appreciated the opening for the organic conversation Archie seemed to want. "When I was maybe twelve, my class joined this program where we each had a pen pal in a similar class in New Jersey. It was a good opportunity to practice my written English. So I suppose that was how I was educated."

"You speak French well too. Or I assume you do, since your accent sounds good, but I'll admit I don't know much French. Did you have to learn when you lived in France?"

"Yes. Although I'd been studying French in school."

A waiter came by with their wine, pausing the conversation. After he left and Archie took a sip from his glass, Archie said, "I know some Greek because I spoke it with my grandparents. That, and we went to Greece every other year or so when I was growing up. My father was fluent, but my mother didn't speak it, so we didn't speak much Greek at home. I took Spanish in school, but it's pretty rusty. So I never really learned to be fluent in another language."

"I'm not sure you need to. They speak English most places."

Archie smiled. He had a great smile, with straight white teeth and eyes that crinkled at the edges. It looked genuine. "Look at us getting to know each other."

"Perish the thought."

"For the first time all day, I feel like we might even pull this off."

"If not, we did have a whirlwind courtship, did we not? Ms. Smalls knows full well I've only been here since July. So we haven't had a great deal of time. Anything we can't answer could be explained away by just not yet having come up in conversation."

Archie sipped his wine. "Yes. That's true."

"And, hey, if we keep getting to know each other, we may even end up in a real relationship."

Archie's face was unreadable. He tilted his head and stared at his plate for a moment. Then he looked up and said, "It wouldn't be the worst thing."

"That's not exactly a ringing endorsement."

"Well, I mean… what do you want?" Archie asked. "Do you want us to just keep faking it? That seems like a lonely prospect to me. We can't just keep living in the house like estranged roommates."

Ondrej found the argument persuasive. Clearly they were attracted to each other. They had enough in common to sustain a conversation. Ondrej still worried sometimes that Archie wasn't always authentic, and he was too good an actor for Ondrej to tell when he was pretending, but he otherwise liked Archie.

"I did have fun this weekend," Ondrej said.

"There you go. Do you think it's possible for us to have fun together out of bed as well?"

Archie looked so earnest that Ondrej couldn't help but smile. "I imagine so."

WHEN they returned home, Archie felt awkward as he tried to decide if he should proposition Ondrej or if it was safe to assume they'd end up in bed together. He watched Ondrej toe off his shoes before Archie took a step forward and said, "I had a nice time tonight."

Ondrej looked up with an eyebrow raised.

Archie was suddenly self-conscious. "I just meant that it was… it was great to spend time with you when we aren't either fucking or talking about business. But forget it. Never mind."

Ondrej took a step toward Archie and said, "No, I don't want to forget it. It was a nice sentiment. I had a good time too."

Archie sighed. "I never know how to act with you," he said, confessing something he'd been holding in all day. "Like, I want you to come upstairs with me and spend the night in my bedroom, but I don't even know how to say that without either sounding lecherous or deceitful."

Ondrej frowned. "Deceitful?"

Archie groaned; maybe the wine had addled his brain or something. He knew he wasn't quite making sense. "Our whole relationship still feels kind of deceitful."

"I know, but…." Ondrej looked away and seemed to find the glass panel in the front door intensely interesting for a moment. Then he said, "Let's just lay it all out on the table, all right? We're still not completely comfortable with each other because we're getting to know each other.

These circumstances are trying. They're strange. But tell me: in this moment, right now, what is it you want?"

Archie wanted to be with Ondrej in every way possible. He wanted to take Ondrej upstairs and make love to him, and then he wanted Ondrej to stay with him in bed for the rest of the night, the week, the month, their lives. It was foolish to feel so invested, but the more Archie got to know Ondrej, the more he liked him. Archie's early interest had been lust-fueled, but he liked spending time with Ondrej out of bed too. It wasn't love, not yet, but Archie thought it could get there if they spent more time together.

But he couldn't say all that to Ondrej. Ondrej needed more convincing. He needed actions, not words. And he clearly wasn't in the same place Archie was yet.

So Archie said, "Right now? I want to have sex with you."

Ondrej nodded slowly. "If we were on a normal date, this would be the part where you invite me back to your place for a glass of wine and a sexual tryst."

"Yes. Those things can still happen. We're already at my place. There's wine in the kitchen."

Ondrej smiled. "The wine would be a pretense. I think we both know what we want here."

Archie wanted to ask, "Do you want me?" but it sounded too needy before he even said the words out loud. "Yes," he said. "Come upstairs with me?"

Ondrej nodded again and stepped forward. He offered his hand, and then he led Archie up the stairs and down the hall to Archie's bedroom.

Once they were there, Archie still wasn't quite sure what to do. He was torn between treating the moment with respect and just tearing off Ondrej's clothes.

He undid his tie and said, "You know, if this keeps happening, you could just move into this bedroom."

Ondrej looked startled, shooting Archie a deer-in-the-headlights look. "You do have a better bed," he said, "but I don't know if I'm quite ready for that."

The depth of Archie's disappointment surprised him, but he said, "Consider it a real offer. I'd like you to spend more nights with me, but only if you want to. So… my door's open, I guess. If you want."

Ondrej stepped toward Archie and put his hands on Archie's waist. "Thank you. I will keep that in mind." He looked away for a brief moment before turning back and catching Archie's gaze. "You're a sweet man under the brusque exterior."

"Oh," Archie said, taken aback. "Thank you. I think. Am I that brusque?"

"I meant it as a compliment. And you're only like that at work when you think your employees are watching. You're full of surprises. I wonder sometimes if the person I'm talking to is the real you or the act you put on for the public."

Archie had at one point lost his grasp on his real self, and he knew that. He didn't always know when he was being genuine and when he was doing what others thought he should do. But he said, "This is the real me now."

Ondrej smiled. "All right." Then he kissed Archie.

Archie kissed him back. He reached up and ran his fingers through Ondrej's hair and held him there as they explored each other's mouths. "I do want you," Archie murmured against Ondrej's mouth. "That's real."

Ondrej reached between them and cupped Archie's hardening cock. "I believe you."

Archie barked out a laugh, because suddenly this all seemed so ridiculous. Ondrej laughed too.

"Sorry," said Ondrej. "That sounded sexier in my head."

"It was sexy. Sorry, I was mostly laughing at myself because I can be so awkward and weird sometimes."

"That's how I know I'm talking to the real you right now." Ondrej kissed Archie again. "You're good at pretending not to be awkward in public. I like you when you're more flabbergasted and less polished."

"Come to bed," Archie said. "Be with me tonight, at least."

"Yes, baby. Yes, I will."

Archie led Ondrej to the bed. He spent the next hour trying to forget that this was fleeting, because the more he touched Ondrej, the more he got lost in Ondrej's flesh, in the sounds he made, in the way he smelled, the more he knew he was in for the big heartache when Ondrej eventually used Archie for his intended purpose and left him.

Chapter Thirteen

ONDREJ had forgotten that his old boss Amy was a vegetarian, so he was somewhat surprised to see that the restaurant she'd picked had no meat dishes on the menu.

As he thought about what to eat, Amy said, "So how are things going with Mr. Tall, Dark, and Handsome?"

He nearly laughed. "We have an interview with an immigration agent tomorrow so she can properly investigate my green card application."

Amy guffawed. "You sound like you're joking. Are you joking?"

"Everyone assures me that my odds of actually getting deported are pretty slim, but no, I'm not joking. An actual agent is coming to the house tomorrow to interview me and Archie to verify that we're actually in love, just like on TV."

"Wow. I didn't think that happened in the real world."

"Normally, it doesn't." Ondrej explained what he'd heard about how CIS processed green card applications and his theory about timing and Archie's high profile. "I mean, based on what I've read online, they would interview everyone if they had the resources, but apparently they only make the effort if you have a suspicious-seeming high-profile marriage with a lot of money involved."

"Ah," said Amy. "But you kind of knew this was a possibility. Hence all the public appearances and schmoopyness in interviews."

"Interviews? What interviews?"

Amy's eyes went wide. "Did you not see the cover story in this month's *Fast Company*? Your husband is one of the leading LGBT CEOs in the country, according to the story. When they interviewed him, he gushed about you all over the page. I'm surprised he didn't show you."

"Really? No, I didn't see it." Archie? Gushing about Ondrej? That seemed out of character. Unless he was acting again. "Guess I'll have to track down a copy."

"It was cute," Amy said. "There's lots of tittering among the ladies in accounts payable too, about how adorable a couple you two make. Some think he's even calmed down since he got married, that he yells less and seems less angry. They credit your influence. There's been some speculation about what happens when you close yourselves into his office."

"Mostly we go over the company's finances."

Amy laughed. "That's the least sexy thing I ever heard."

Ondrej debated whether to tell Amy—who had become his friend, even before he stopped working for her—about the fact that he and Archie were now sleeping together most nights. He ruled against it; he still wasn't sure what to make of his relationship with Archie.

After they ordered food, Amy said, "This relationship is actually a good thing for the company, believe it or not."

"What do you mean?"

Amy looked around. They were still within a few blocks of the Katsaros offices, so there might have been employees within hearing distance. She lowered her head and said softly, "Cone of silence, okay?" She gestured with her hands, miming a cone around them.

"Of course."

"The news media always had nice things to say about Alexander Katsaros. He was charming and handsome and everything you wanted as the public face of a company. But he was also kind of a dick."

"Yeah?" Ondrej leaned forward. This didn't surprise him much, but he was interested to hear about the man without the filter of Archie's fond recollections.

"His management style bordered on verbal abuse sometimes, I swear. He had kind of an old-school attitude, I guess, especially toward women. He yelled and lost his temper a lot. He'd scold female employees in front of the entire office, even if their infractions were minor. I once submitted a report that had one total off by three cents, and he lectured me about accuracy for a good ten minutes while the entire department looked on."

"Wow."

"Archie took over just in time, because people were starting to lose faith in Alexander's ability to lead anyone. Productivity was down, and some departments were deliberately slowing down work. It's hard to be motivated to do a good job when you believe nothing you ever do will be good enough."

Ondrej nodded. "Such an American thing, that. Working your employees to the bone and then telling them they're not doing enough."

"Yes, well, that is how Alexander Katsaros operated most of the time. He wanted his employees to be afraid of him, I assume because he thought that would keep them in line."

"From what I've seen, Archie's pretty hard on his people too. The way he is now is him being *less* mean? I'd hate to have seen him before we met."

Amy nodded. "That's just it, though. I've known Archie since I started working at the company. He showed me around and got me oriented, and he helped make my promotion happen. He was always a super sweet guy. So I know that when he's being hard on his employees, it's an act."

Ondrej already suspected the same, but he said, "Really?"

"Sure. I mean, you've spent plenty of time with him by now. You know he's a marshmallow inside."

Because they were friends, Ondrej said, "Honestly, I am not always sure what is real and what is an act."

Amy seemed to find that interesting, tilting her head and nodding knowingly. "I'll tell you this, then. Archie is nothing like his father. He postures a lot in front of his employees, yeah, but he's much more reserved. When you get him just talking, he comes across like a nice guy. Alexander never had that vibe."

It was true that Archie at home was nothing like Archie in the office, and Ondrej had been struggling to reconcile these two people. He liked the Archie he had casual dinners with, whom he talked to late at night when they were lying in bed, who just that morning had laughed in the shower when Ondrej had surprised him by sliding into it with him.

"He doesn't want to lay off anyone," Ondrej said, realizing Amy was probably right.

"What?"

Ondrej looked at Amy straight on for the first time since this conversation began. "He doesn't want to lay anyone off. I keep telling him the easiest way to save money is to streamline, meaning anyone who isn't adding value to their department should be let go, but Archie isn't hearing me. He wants to streamline without anyone losing his job."

"See?" Amy crossed her arms over her chest. "Marshmallow."

Their food arrived and Ondrej stared at the green plate before him. So much lettuce. He sighed and picked up his fork.

"I think the issue for Archie," Amy said, "is that he doesn't really know how to handle his employees, so he does what he thinks he should rather than what his instincts tell him to do. And you have to understand, it was always clear he worshipped his father. I think their relationship cooled toward the end, but Alexander could do no wrong. You can see it in the way Archie acts. He does what he thinks his father would do. But that's not who Archie is."

Ondrej ate his salad silently for a few moments, taking that in. Probably he should have a talk with Archie about honesty and company policy. Really, though, Ondrej wanted to know about honesty and their relationship; he wanted to know where he stood with Archie, and he didn't have a good sense of that. They had mutual sexual attraction in abundance, but what else did they have?

What else did Ondrej want?

"I keep telling him to change his approach to dealing with employees. Maybe if he sees people respond differently to a softer approach, he'll be more persuaded. I'll talk to him about the layoffs too."

Amy frowned. "That was the other thing I wanted to mention. I heard he gave you an office."

"You know as well as I do that it's my money keeping the company afloat. Archie agreed to let me use the office whenever it strikes me, and I have limited access to the daily workings of the company and can sit in on board meetings."

"Do you think that will affect your relationship at home?"

Would it? Ondrej hadn't really considered it, but probably. If there was one thing Ondrej was concerned about, it was the upcoming argument over money, particularly as it pertained to spending on future Katsaros projects. Archie had the power to bankrupt them both. "I'm sure we'll argue about money, but—"

"And what is it you expect to happen at home?"

Ondrej let out an exasperated sigh. "I don't know. I like him. But we're doing this backwards. If I had just met him and we were dating like normal people, I'd be open to whatever, like yeah, maybe he's the one, but maybe we'll break up in two months. But we're already married." And truth be told, Ondrej feared getting stuck. If things didn't work out with Archie, Ondrej would still have to live in his house, at least until he finished the work to become a US citizen. And what if staying with Archie prevented Ondrej from meeting the person he was supposed to be with? Not that he even believed in fate, per se, but this felt like slamming the door on possibility.

"I guess the decision you have to make is whether you want to keep up the fraud or try to give the marriage a go."

"I just don't know." It wasn't entirely true; Ondrej had decided at some point during their sex marathon weekend that if this was what marriage was like, he'd be more than willing to try. Because he loved being with Archie that way, in the safety of that huge bed, where they just laughed and talked and had sex until they were sore. The weekend had been magical. The reality of the work week, less so.

"Because if you wanted to forge a real relationship with him, meddling in office affairs is probably not the way to do it. He'll resent you for getting involved."

"If he doesn't already."

"Well." Amy frowned. "It's worth thinking about. I mean, I know couples whose marriages fell apart when they started working together. Your relationship is even more fragile than that."

Amy was right. Ondrej might already have set up an impossible situation. He cursed.

"I'm going to assume that was a Czech swear," Amy said cheerfully.

"This is so bizarre. I thought I knew what I was getting into, but there are all these angles I hadn't considered. And the worst part is that I wanted to stay here, in New York, but I've been cooped up at home most of the time since the wedding." And hadn't the point of coming to New York been to explore sex and men without his family being privy to any of it? How had he stumbled into a committed relationship? None of this had gone the way he'd planned. "And if this immigration interview goes badly, I'll have to go back to Prague anyway, and then what the hell was the point of all this?"

"Guess you'll have to nail the interview."

Ondrej sighed. He figured she was kidding. "Thanks, Amy."

ONDREJ swung by the office after lunch. Archie was busy but happy for the distraction.

"Am I meddling too much?" Ondrej asked.

"What?"

"You allowed me to get involved with the management of my investment in the company, but do you think I'm meddling in the company's affairs too much? Am I overstepping my boundaries?"

Archie didn't know how to answer the question. He mumbled something to stall but then said, "Well, I'll admit, I'm enough of a control freak where my company is concerned that I don't exactly enjoy having someone else tell me how to do things, but I value your insights."

"So if I do something that pisses you off, you'll tell me."

"Sure." Archie still didn't understand this line of questioning. "Where is this coming from?"

Ondrej sighed and dropped into one of the guest chairs. "I just don't want you to resent me."

"Why would I?"

Ondrej gazed past Archie out the window that overlooked Broadway. "You just said you're a control freak. And I'm trying to impose a lot of change on the company, because I am too. But we have to live together, so I…." Ondrej shook his head.

Archie took a moment to watch and think. He was generally happy with how their personal relationship was progressing; it felt like they'd passed over some kind of threshold. So he said, "You're worried that resentment at work will bleed over into resentment at home."

Ondrej looked up and met Archie's gaze. He opened and closed his mouth a couple of times, but then he said, "Yes."

Lord, this situation was complicated in so many ways Archie hadn't anticipated. "Then I promise to let you know if you've pushed me too far. At work and at home. Okay?"

Ondrej nodded. "I just think…." He bit his lip and frowned. "I just want honesty. If we're going to build something real, we need to be honest with each other."

"Of course. Is that what you want? Something real?" Archie held his breath as he waited for a response.

"I want to see if it's possible," Ondrej said.

That was a little disappointing. Archie reflected that perhaps many days of good sex had clouded his brain and made him think there was more between them than there actually was. Ondrej hadn't closed the door, but his face reiterated now that he and Archie were not in the same place. Maybe they never would be. Archie's inclination was to laugh it off, to pretend that didn't bother him, but Ondrej was right. Honesty was called for if they even had a chance.

"All right. Here's how I feel right now. I like spending time with you," Archie said. "I like you a lot, in fact. Maybe it'll never quite click with us, but I want to try too."

Ondrej nodded. "Good. So be honest with me. No more acting, at least not with me. Okay?"

"All right." Archie wasn't sure what he was promising, though he supposed he had told Ondrej straight out that a lot of his public persona was a façade. He took a deep breath. "I have to put on a mask when I do public appearances, we both know that, but I want to take it off when I'm with you. When we're alone in the house. When we're behind closed doors. So I promise I won't act when I'm alone with you, okay?"

Ondrej nodded slowly. "Yes. That's… I'm grateful."

Archie didn't want Ondrej's gratitude, though. He wanted affection. This still felt like so many business transactions. But Archie kept his mouth shut.

Ondrej stood. "Okay. I'm gonna head out. I want to prepare for the board meeting Friday, but I think I'm better off not being in the office while I think over some things."

"Sure. Whatever you need. You can use the office at home, if you like."

Ondrej's eyes crinkled at the edges and his lips turned up slightly. Not quite a smile, but it was something. "All right. I may just do that. Thank you, Archie."

"You're welcome."

Then Ondrej smiled for real and left the office. Archie wanted to call him back and make him smile more, but by the time he opened his mouth to do so, Ondrej was too far down the hall.

Chapter Fourteen

NANCY Smalls was a petite middle-aged woman with frizzy dyed-blonde hair. She smiled widely as Ondrej let her into the foyer.

"I didn't know houses like this still existed!" she said as she looked around.

"Archie's mother's family," Ondrej said. "They're descended from one of the old New York families, but I can't remember which offhand."

"Archie? Oh, Archimedes. Of course. And where is your husband?"

"He's in the living room. Follow me, please."

Ondrej led Nancy Smalls into the formal living room, a room that, as far as Ondrej could tell, Archie never used. Archie had slipped Hildy a little extra to come by and be thorough about dusting the day before, so at least it looked like someone had been in the room more recently than 1948. The furniture was old but well cared for. Quite a bit of junk cluttered the room: old family heirlooms and antique doodads and the sort of stuff that decorated the living quarters of wealthy people who didn't know what to do with all their money.

Archie stood as they entered. "I'm Archimedes Katsaros," he said to Ms. Smalls. "Welcome to our home."

They'd staged this meeting the night before, everything from their clothes—Ondrej wore a windowpane plaid shirt and tie, while Archie had pulled a conservative navy sweater over his office shirt—to offering Nancy a grandiose midcentury modern armchair while Archie and Ondrej sat beside each other on an ostentatious sofa facing her. They all sat now, and Ondrej tried to wait patiently while Nancy pulled out a notebook and a pen, though he felt like he was crawling out of his skin.

She clicked the pen and said, "So. I suppose you know why I'm here."

Archie nodded. "I feel bad that you had to come all the way uptown. I know how the situation looks, and I will admit that the end of Ondrej's visa forced us to marry sooner than we might have otherwise, but that was only because I couldn't live without him and didn't want him to move back to Prague." Archie put his arm around Ondrej.

This was all planned. What wasn't planned was the way Archie leaned closer and put his forehead against Ondrej's temple. It was an affectionate gesture, likely born of the intimacy they'd been sharing at night all week. Ondrej closed his eyes, briefly blocking out Nancy Smalls, to just feel the warmth of Archie's body nearby.

It wasn't love. But it wasn't indifference, either.

Archie sat back up and leaned away, though he kept his arm along the back of the sofa, where he could brush his fingertips across the back of Ondrej's head. Ondrej really liked that too.

Nancy Smalls clicked her pen again. "You understand that there's quite a bit of marriage fraud. It's less likely with gay couples, I will admit, but you have to understand how it looks." She sighed. "The USCIS is cracking down on green card marriages due to an increase in fraud relating to immigration. It's a problem we haven't had the resources to fully address yet, but my boss insisted I come meet you. Given that Mr. Kovac's visa expired so close to your wedding, it was suspicious, and there's a great deal of money at stake here too."

Ondrej frowned at that. He wasn't surprised she'd run their financials as part of the investigation, but he hated the probe into his affairs. He wasn't just bothered by the fact that the financials made the marriage look more suspect, with good reason; the invasion of privacy made him uncomfortable. Somehow he hadn't anticipated this when he'd agreed to get married.

"How did you meet?" she asked.

She posed the question casually, as if she were asking at a cocktail party, but she clicked her pen a few more times and then wrote something in the notebook propped on her lap, poised to take down the answer.

That made Ondrej self-conscious, but he said, "When I arrived in the States, I needed a job to maintain my work visa, so I took an internship at Katsaros Holdings. A friend of mine from back home knew one of the managers there."

"I came through the offices where Ondrej was working one afternoon, and our eyes met across the sea of cubicles. I swear, it was like lightning struck." Archie sounded so earnest, even Ondrej was briefly convinced. "So I asked him to dinner, and the rest is history. Although I had to let him go, because dating an employee is clearly a conflict of interest. Thus Ondrej's work visa would expire unless he could find other work, which he didn't. We had this crazy whirlwind relationship, and just when he had resigned himself to going back to the Czech Republic, I asked him to marry me."

"And how has married life been treating you, Mr. Kovac?" Ms. Smalls asked.

"Lovely, so far. I mean, it's still all very new." Ondrej hooked his arm around Archie's torso. "But just last week, he took me to a charity gala that was more spectacular than anything I'd seen before." There. That sounded convincing.

Ms. Smalls nodded. "Look, I know how much you guys must hate this, but you have to understand how much fraud crosses my desk every day. It's not at all unusual for a foreigner to pay an American an exorbitant sum of money in exchange for a green card marriage. Nor is it unusual for a foreigner to trick an American into thinking they're in love so that he can get a green card." She looked pointedly at Ondrej when she said this.

"I can assure you, I have been nothing but honest with Archie since we started seeing each other," Ondrej said. That was true, at least.

Ms. Smalls wrote something down in her notebook. "I could ask you a bunch of probing questions designed to ascertain how well you really know each other. But you both live in this house?"

"Yes," said Ondrej.

"A bit formal, no?" Ms. Smalls asked.

"Just this room," said Archie. "We really only use this room to entertain guests. The TV and video games and things are all downstairs in the den. That seems to be Ondrej's favorite room."

Ondrej shrugged. "There's a lot of American TV I missed out on before I moved here."

"Can I see that room?" Ms. Smalls asked.

Archie hesitated but then nodded and stood. Ondrej and Ms. Smalls followed him across the foyer to the staircase at the back of the house. As they went down the stairs, Ms. Smalls asked, "Mr. Katsaros, your own father was an immigrant, wasn't he?"

"Yes. He came here from Greece in the sixties." Archie made a little sound that Ondrej couldn't quite interpret, but it sounded like resignation. He went on, "He was working for a real estate firm on the Upper West Side when he met my mother. Her family was selling an apartment in the Dakota. To hear my mother tell it, he charmed her socks off."

"Romantic," Ms. Smalls deadpanned.

"Mother's family was vigilant about gold diggers. I had an uncle with a spoiled witch of a trophy wife about whom my grandmother never had anything nice to say. But my grandparents adored my father. If my parents' relationship had been anything but loving, there's no way my grandparents would have allowed the wedding to take place. And sure, my father used a great deal of my mother's money to buy property and get Katsaros Holdings off the ground, but the whole family has a long history of real estate speculation. It was all done with my grandparents' blessing, and my parents had a wonderful relationship until my mother passed away from breast cancer when I was a teenager." Archie let out a breath. "Most of my mother's family is gone now.

But I can't help but think I'd disappoint them if I did anything but marry for love."

Ondrej wondered how much of that was true—likely most of it, if what Ondrej already knew of Archie was anything to go by—and he realized how much Archie must hate the lies he was telling. Probably it had been eating at him all along. Ondrej briefly felt guilty but knew also that Archie had entered this arrangement with his eyes open.

They arrived in the den, and Ms. Smalls looked around. This room was the only one in the house with more modern furniture. The white sofa was a little precious, but the big blue blanket Ondrej snuggled under when the AC became too intense was casually tossed over the back of the sofa, and the blue throw pillows were off-kilter. Ondrej had left the case for the movie he'd been watching the night before out on the TV stand; it was some political thriller that hadn't been that good, or else Ondrej hadn't yet grasped American politics enough to understand it. The rug on the floor between the sofa and the TV was also just slightly off, and there was a stack of magazines on the coffee table that would have toppled over if anyone bumped into the table. This room looked lived-in, in other words, unlike the formal living room.

"Mr. Kovac is independently wealthy, is he not? I noted that you recently opened a joint bank account. Mr. Kovac also made a substantial transfer of funds into a Katsaros Holdings account."

"I'm investing in my husband's company," Ondrej said. "Archie assures me he has a plan to improve and expand." Ondrej chose his words carefully, unsure how much Nancy Smalls knew already. "I figured Katsaros Holdings would be a good place to put my money. If the company carries out the plans Archie has shown me, I should see a substantial return on my investment. I know that sounds dry, but that was all the motivation there."

"Not because Katsaros Holdings needed the money?" Ms. Smalls asked.

"It did. I won't claim ignorance there," Ondrej said, his veins suddenly icy. They'd rehearsed this part a little too, just in case, and decided that Ondrej playing innocent as far as finances went would only serve to make him look like a patsy. He threw his arm around Archie. "I believe in Archie, though."

"I put him on the company's board of directors," Archie said. "He's a nonvoting member, for obvious reasons, but he has access to company financial records. Everything is transparent. He wanted to invest his money of his own volition, so I'm letting him do it honestly."

Ms. Smalls nodded and wrote something on her fucking pad of paper.

"We get how it looks," Ondrej said.

She nodded. "You've likely seen the tabloid rumors that this is a green card marriage."

Ondrej and Archie both gasped. Ondrej had no idea tabloids had reported on them. He'd made a point not to indulge in any searches for himself online, not wanting to know whatever nonsense that reporter he'd met at the gala would write, so he had no idea he and Archie were even a subject worthy of tabloid speculation. He broke out in a cold sweat and looked at Archie for help.

"Tabloids?" Archie spat. "Of course there are rumors, but I assure you—"

She held up her hand. "My boss pressured me to investigate. There is also a lot of red tape here. It may take extra time, perhaps as long as two years, to process the green card request."

Ondrej frowned. He'd been expecting to stay married to Archie for a year. He understood the implication here that they'd stall the proceedings as a kind of waiting period to make sure Ondrej didn't get his green card and then immediately get a divorce. By then it would legally be too late to investigate the fraud, but everyone would know. That made the USCIS look bad. "I can't be deported in that time, can I? I don't want to be separated from Archie. And my family back home is not exactly supportive of… well." He gestured between himself and Archie.

"You can't be deported while the application is still pending. Are you worried about going back to Prague? Is that why you came to the States?" Ms. Small asked.

Ondrej nodded. "My mother was putting pressure on me to marry a woman, but I just… couldn't. It's literally the Old World where my family lives. They haven't come around to the idea of healthy gay relationships. When I called my family to tell them about Archie, my mother screamed and my father threatened to disinherit me. So there's that." That was true too, though the threat was meaningless, since his parents couldn't touch the money he'd inherited from his grandparents. The situation would be trickier if he lost everything he'd invested in Katsaros Holdings, but he still held out some hope that he and Archie could save the company. The conversation with his father had been unpleasant but surprisingly calm. Ondrej had simply repeated what he told his mother; his father had said he knew already and added he would take Ondrej off the will if he continued in this foolishness.

At long last, Nancy Smalls's poker face dissolved into something like sympathy. "Well. I think I've seen what I need to. You two have what seems like a happy relationship. Like I said, I wouldn't expect your change of status to happen quickly, but I'll pass on my recommendation that it be approved."

Ondrej wanted to cheer. He couldn't keep the smile off his face in the burst of relief he felt. "Thank you, Ms. Smalls."

"I'll show you out," Archie said.

Ondrej waited in the den for Archie to return, which he did a few minutes later with a broad grin on his face. "We did it," he said. "We totally nailed that."

"We did, yes."

Archie gave Ondrej a tight hug, which Ondrej wriggled out of, embarrassed by the burst of affection. He wasn't sure what to say on such an occasion. "I won't be deported right away," Ondrej said.

"I'm glad you get to stay," Archie said.

"Me too. Thanks for your help, Archie. I still kind of can't believe we pulled that off."

Archie laughed. "I think part of her wanted to believe us. But I get it. The department would look inept if someone this high profile pulled off a fraud."

"Well, given that this *is* a fraud, her department *is* kind of inept."

Archie pulled away and took a step back. "Right."

"Come on, Archie. Don't look like I just kicked your dog. You know what I mean. I care about you, but that's not why we got married."

"Right," Archie said. His whole face shut down, as if it had turned to stone.

Ondrej realized he'd said the wrong thing. "That isn't to say we can't—"

"No, you're right. It's all fake." He pulled his phone from this pocket and glanced at the display. "I've got six texts from Marketa. I better get back to the office. I'll see you later, Ondrej." Then he left.

Ondrej's heart sank. He knew he'd hurt Archie. But surely Archie knew… but no, things had changed, hadn't they?

Well, no matter. This afternoon's interview had given Ondrej more time to figure out what to do next.

Chapter Fifteen

ARCHIE'S heart beat erratically as he walked into the Friday morning board meeting. He'd slept without Ondrej the night before for the first time all week. It had been his decision, though; he'd told Ondrej he wanted to sleep alone.

Because Archie had gotten involved emotionally, in ways he hadn't completely expected to. Sure, he'd thought Ondrej might come around to the idea of a real relationship eventually, but Archie himself hadn't thought he'd fall so hard so fast. So he'd made Ondrej sleep in his own room the night before because their whole relationship was a fraud and Archie needed some distance before he let his heart really get stomped on.

Because if Ondrej still thought the foundation of their relationship was merely a business arrangement, what the hell was the point? If he was just going to leave when he got his green card, why should Archie get invested?

Archie walked into the boardroom and took his place at the head of the table. He greeted a few of the other board members amiably. Dan Preston, Archie's one relative on the board, walked over as Archie was arranging his notes, and slapped him on the back. He'd been by Archie's office earlier that morning to say he wanted to call for a vote on selling off parts of the company—he had a potential buyer, he claimed—and no amount of Archie asking him to postpone until after the efficiency proposal would dissuade him. Archie smiled at his cousin, but his stomach churned. Dan walked around the table, shaking hands with the other board members and charming them in a way Archie wasn't sure he could compete with.

Just when Archie was really starting to lose hope, Ondrej walked in, which didn't do much to bolster Archie's confidence.

Archie stood and gestured to the seat he'd designated for Ondrej. As Ondrej walked to it and pulled it away from the table, Archie said, "Let's call this meeting to order." Once everyone was settled and their attention was on Archie, he began to speak again. "Allow me to introduce my husband, Ondrej Kovac. As you are aware, I've given Ondrej a nonvoting position on the board, making him privy to financial considerations within the company. I anticipated that a few of you might object, which is why Ondrej doesn't have a vote, but he is permitted to attend meetings and give his opinion where appropriate."

The assembled board members glanced at each other or stared at Ondrej, but no one said anything. Ondrej met Archie's gaze but also stayed silent.

Archie got the meeting started, briefing everyone on relevant business. Then he turned the floor over to the board of directors: eight minority shareholders who had come on board under the reign of Alexander Katsaros—all of them men; no one said he hadn't been sexist—and whom Archie hadn't seen fit to remove. Mostly they let him run the company at his discretion, but sitting on the board made them feel important. Or something like that; Archie didn't much understand the board's purpose if they didn't stop Alexander from running the company into the ground. But no matter; this was the way business was conducted. If they were content to sit idly by as the Katsaros men made decisions, that was just fine with Archie.

Unfortunately, there was still Dan Preston, who said, "You're all aware of how dire the situation has become. We're all losing money, more every quarter. Which is why I've put together the following proposal." He produced a sheaf of paper and started handing out stapled-together packets. "I understand Archie is about to give us a counterproposal, so I don't expect we'll vote on a course of action today, but I do want the board to consider *all* of our options. Here, I've outlined a proposal in which we sell 40 percent of our assets to the Cochrane Group. Bernadette Cochrane herself is interested in the sale. Deal's off the table unless we include certain properties, which I've outlined on page four."

Ondrej listened quietly as Dan spoke. Archie listened too, and though the proposal angered him—most of the properties on Dan's list were Katsaros Holdings' most profitable, and this proposal would effectively pull the rug out from under the company—he also mentally rehearsed what he planned to say. When at last it was his turn to speak again, he cleared his throat.

"Dan's right," Archie said. "I do have a counterproposal, because I think this one is terrible. You all know as well as Dan does that if we sell off this much of the company, even for the number Dan quotes, the company will sink faster than the *Titanic*."

Archie took a deep breath and tried to find some kind of center to hold on to. He glanced at Ondrej, who looked at him intently. Archie wanted Ondrej's support, wanted something he could grab in his hands. Ondrej was there, but he was too far away to touch.

"I'll be blunt," Archie continued. "The numbers my father was passing to you all were not accurate. You must know by now that Katsaros Holdings is farther in the hole than he let on. Due to inefficiency, the financial disaster in Greece where he still had money tied up, and mismanagement on nearly every level, we're floundering. Mr. Preston's solution is a tidy one, but one I believe will bankrupt the company, and frankly, I do not intend to let that happen. I've been working hard to restore Katsaros to its proud tradition, as you know. I believe that rather than selling off profitable assets, we can make cuts within the organization. Mr. Kovac has gathered reports from some of the managers to explain what cuts we can make. The goal is to streamline our operations so that we stop bleeding money and perhaps even profit again in the short term."

Archie hadn't consulted much with Ondrej yet. He hadn't wanted to rock the boat at home, where things seemed to be going well. Well, they'd been going well until yesterday, when Ondrej had made it clear this was all still pretend.

They were not merely pretending to save a company, though, so Archie went through the planks of his proposal, which included laying off a dozen employees. "I'm willing to sell assets, but not most of the properties Mr. Preston has suggested. Instead, we should consider selling perhaps a few of the Upper East Side properties, which aren't as lucrative as they once were. If not Cochrane, I'm certain we will find other buyers. There is no shortage of people wishing to invest in real estate in this city. The income from those sales can then be invested in new ventures that will turn a greater profit." Archie went on, slowly going through the rest of his proposal. When he finished, he said, "Mr. Kovac, do you have anything to add?"

Ondrej nodded and stood. "I know you're all deeply skeptical of me, but I think this company would benefit from an outsider opinion. You're all clearly intelligent, but you may be too close to this situation or too invested in the late Mr. Katsaros's legacy." He glared at Dan briefly. Archie imagined Ondrej was thinking the board was too invested, save for Dan. Ondrej went on, "Let me tell you what I see."

Ondrej was impressive. Even in his accented English, he communicated clearly, laying out a plan even more radical than Archie's, but one intended to promote efficiency while still keeping the company's most valuable properties. He concluded by saying, "But these are just suggestions. Mr. Katsaros's plans are sound as well, and I agree that would be a good direction to head in. The one bone of contention between us is the Eagles stadium project."

"It's a good investment," Archie said. "And it's hardly unprecedented. The other recent stadium projects in the city have done well."

"They have, yes, but five years from the point we're at now. Katsaros may not have that kind of time before things get dire. And we all know what a quagmire the

Atlantic Yards project turned out to be. I know you want this, Archie, but let's consider this rationally and realistically."

Archie didn't want to argue with Ondrej in front of the board, and he was a little annoyed Ondrej had disagreed with him, so he said, "We'll discuss and return to the issue at the next board meeting. I put together a report on the stadium project if you'd all care to read it." Archie stood and began to hand out the booklets Marketa had helped him make.

Ondrej nodded and sat back down, apparently satisfied with that response.

The board spent the next half hour debating the planks of the respective improvement plans. The consensus opinion leaned toward Archie's least radical approach, but two members and Dan expressed doubts about the profitability of the Eagles stadium project. Debate was mostly calm—this board never got riled up, from what Archie could tell, and seemed to prefer a passive-aggressive approach to an argumentative one—but it became clear they were not very close to being able to vote.

In the end, though, the board gave Archie the green light to proceed with the first plank of his plan while everyone agreed to study Dan's proposal and the stadium project report. The day of reckoning would come at the next board meeting, which at least gave Archie some time to better counter Dan's ambitious proposal.

Archie stood and wrapped up the meeting, feeling pretty good about how it had gone. Once it adjourned and everyone got up to leave, Archie left the room. Ondrej didn't catch up with him until he was nearly back at his office.

"What's the rush?" Ondrej said.

"The meeting was over." Archie walked into his office. The truth was that he always wanted to get out of those meetings as quickly as possible, though he thought leaving abruptly lent him a certain air of authority. There was no need to linger and chitchat.

Ondrej followed him into the office and closed the door as he came in. "All right. Are you angry? Did I overstep in my presentation?"

Archie sat with a sigh. "No. I'm sorry." He rubbed his forehead. "Look, you've probably put together that I try to keep up a stoic exterior for the board, but it's hard sometimes. My father could be a hardass, and he was good at keeping those meetings short and sweet. I have such a hard time asserting myself that way."

"I had a notion some of your blustering in front of the employees was an act." Ondrej smiled. "I could see what you were doing with the board."

"I want them to respect me."

"They do. Or they will, once you show you can turn the company around. You'll have to stand up to Dan, of course, but I thought you did a fine job in there just now."

Archie didn't want to display his crisis of confidence too brightly, so he bit his lip and nodded.

"Are you upset?" Ondrej asked.

"I hate board meetings."

"I can see why."

They sat in silence. Archie glanced at his computer monitor and saw he'd gotten a dozen or so e-mails during the meeting.

The thing was, Archie *was* upset. He felt childish, but a part of him wanted to scream. He doubted he'd be able to fix the company before Dan found a bigger buyer—though Cochrane was one of only a half-dozen

real estate firms who owned more of the city than
Katsaros—even if the board agreed to his changes and
even with Ondrej's money, which was distressing him.
His family's legacy was on the line, not to mention his
own livelihood, so failure wasn't an option, but it sure
seemed like a possibility.

And this was not to mention that his longing for
Ondrej had become a palpable thing, and having Ondrej
be right there but not really his was torture.

"Do you want me to leave?" Ondrej asked.

Archie both wanted desperately for Ondrej to stay
and for him to get the hell away. He said, "Yes. I have
work to do."

"Can I take you to lunch later?"

"Better not." Archie wanted to explain himself but
was afraid to speak, or to make himself emotionally
vulnerable enough to let Ondrej hurt him more.

But Ondrej frowned. "You *are* mad about the
board meeting."

"It's not about the board meeting."

"Then what is it? Because you're obviously upset
about something. You slept alone last night and you've
barely spoken to me all day."

"This isn't the time or place for—"

"Are you still upset about the interview yesterday?
Look, I'm sorry if I said something that—"

Archie waved his hand. He'd had enough. If
Ondrej was going to pursue this, he'd get an earful. "Do
you want to know what the problem is? You and I have
a fake relationship. We barely know each other, and
we're perpetrating a fraud. Yesterday I lied to an agent
of the federal government. I've never been completely
comfortable with this arrangement, but I did it because
I thought it was best for me and my company."

"I know the situation is strange, but—"

"The worst part is that I'm really falling for you. The more time I spend with you, the more I like you. So when you reiterated that this is all a fraud, which it is, it only made me realize that it's probably better to put some distance between us before I get in too deep, you know? Because if all this is a joke to you—"

"It's not a joke, Archie."

The way Ondrej's voice cut through Archie's speech brought him up short. "Well, it's certainly not a funny one."

"No." Ondrej looked down for a moment and then said, "It's proximity. Sex. I don't know. We like each other. We respect each other, even, I'd say. We're not in love, no, but I thought maybe—"

"You know what else? You don't really need me. You could find a job and get another work visa and work your way toward becoming a citizen. There are other paths to staying in this country legally. But if you left me, I'd—" Archie held his fist to his mouth. This had been his greatest fear, one he was afraid even to voice. But he'd been thinking it ever since the meeting with Nancy Smalls. Ondrej really *didn't* need Archie. But Archie sure as hell needed Ondrej. And not even for his money; Archie needed Ondrej in his bed, in his life, by his side, bottom line.

"You'd what? If I left, what would you do, Archie?"

"Forget it. It's too confusing. It's too hard." Archie felt exposed. He leaned forward and put his head in his hands.

"Archie, I—"

But Archie was done. "I don't want to discuss this right now. If you haven't noticed, it's the middle of a work day. I've got work I need to get done so that I don't go bankrupt and lose everything. So if you don't mind."

Ondrej stood. "I'll just go home, then."

"Yeah, I think you'd better."

Ondrej left and closed the door again as he did. Archie silently thanked him; now he could lose his mind in peace. It occurred to him that he almost wanted Ondrej more than he wanted the company to succeed, and if he could go back in time and keep those two things from getting so tangled up, he would. Instead, he had to deal with the reality that he only had Ondrej because his company was about to go belly-up. Ondrej, however, was much more than fish food, at least to Archie, and not just because he was hot and good in bed. No, Archie could see himself falling in love with Ondrej and having a real relationship in which they built a life together and lived happily ever after.

But that was a fantasy.

So Archie gave himself five minutes to fall apart behind closed doors. Then he slipped into his private restroom, splashed cold water on his face, and got back to work.

Chapter Sixteen

A STRAINED few days passed in which Archie mostly avoided Ondrej. Ondrej had taken to sleeping in his own room again, which Archie regretted, but he thought it might be the right move under the circumstances.

He was in the kitchen one evening when Ondrej finally confronted him.

"Can I ask what the hell is going on?"

Archie busied himself with adjusting the lids on the Tupperware containers he was about to put in the microwave. "What are you talking about?"

"You've been hiding from me for days. You're not answering my calls when you're in the office. You blow me off when I try to talk to you. What, exactly, is going on that you feel like you have to act this way? Did I do something?"

Archie couldn't think of how best to respond. He stared at the two containers before him—one with leftover chicken, the other with leftover vegetables and rice—and tried to come up with something more concrete than the fact that being in this house with Ondrej was making him feel so out of sorts.

"You were right," Archie said. "I don't know why I thought we could have a real relationship. It's all a fraud. I know it'll be strange, but I think we should go back to just being roommates until your green card comes through. And I know that could be a while, so…."

"Are you joking?" Ondrej stepped over to the counter, standing about three feet from Archie, and pressed his palm into the granite top. He frowned. "No, you're not joking. I don't… what happened? I don't understand."

It frustrated Archie that Ondrej was playing dumb, because he knew as well as Archie what he'd said. "Look, you were right, when we finished our meeting with Nancy Smalls. It's a fraud relationship. I don't know why we feel like we have to pretend otherwise. Or why we have to pretend at all, since you clearly don't need my help. But I'm done pretending."

Ondrej balked. "So that's it? It's over just like that."

Archie shrugged. "Sure seems like that's what you want. I mean, why even bother staying with me when you could just get another work visa anyway?"

Ondrej's eyes went wide. "Is that what this is about?"

Archie knew he was being dramatic and probably waltzing right over some invisible line marking the edge of reasonable behavior, but he felt too raw to rein it in. He wanted Ondrej. He was falling in love with Ondrej. And to watch Ondrej stand there so impassively was killing him. "I don't…. I get that it's hard to find a job in the city right now, that you'd been out of work long enough they would have deported you if we hadn't gotten married, but now you technically have a job at Katsaros, even if you aren't drawing a salary. I could sign the fucking paperwork. Then we can put this whole sham marriage behind us. Isn't that what you want?"

Ondrej lifted his hand and slammed it back down on the countertop. "No, that's not what I want. And I only want that job because I'm married to you. I thought we were, I don't know, moving toward some kind of arrangement."

"Arrangement?" What the hell? This wasn't just some kind of mutual sexual agreement. This was a marriage. And if Ondrej wasn't willing to take it seriously, then Archie was done. He had to back away before he got too entangled emotionally. "It's not a fucking arrangement, Ondrej."

"Then what is it?"

Archie couldn't think of how to explain it. "It's not…. This stopped being just a business *arrangement* for me a long time ago, Ondrej. I know I was probably more invested than you were, but I've always been attracted to you, and when it turned out we had some things in common and could talk? Well, I started to think we might have something real between us. But that's ridiculous, right? I'm fucking delusional. I've been single too long, I've had too much *bullshit* in my life the last year, and I can't even think straight anymore."

Archie knew it was garbled. He knew he probably wasn't making sense or properly conveying what he needed Ondrej to know. But Ondrej also just stood there, looking flabbergasted.

"Archie, I…."

"Forget it." Archie shoved both containers into the microwave and hit the Reheat button.

Ondrej put his hands on his hips and grimaced. "I'm not great at expressing myself sometimes, especially if I don't know the English words, but I don't know where you got the idea that—"

"I know, right? How fucking stupid am I?"

Ondrej dropped his arms and grunted. "Will you let me finish? You had no idea what I was about to say."

"Fine."

"Fine. I was going to say, I don't know where you got this idea that you're more invested than I am. I want this to work."

"You want it to work so you can get your green card, and if you get some good sex out of the *arrangement*, then bonus, right?"

"Sure," Ondrej said with a shrug.

"I don't want you to leave, but maybe it's better if you do, if that's your attitude."

"Archie, I…. I mean, is it the money that makes you want me to stay? I know you need it for the company, and if I were to leave…."

"That's not what this is about," Archie said through his teeth. The comment was a stab in the gut, and not one he wanted to dignify with further speech. He'd laid out his feelings, and if Ondrej couldn't understand how Archie felt, then Archie was done trying to argue.

The microwave beeped, so Archie pulled the containers out. The hot plastic sizzled against his skin, but he didn't care. He flipped the tops off both containers. He grabbed a plate and dumped food onto it. He tossed the containers in the sink and picked up his plate. "I'm going to go eat in the office. Don't follow me. I'd like to be alone for a bit."

"All right."

With that, Archie strode out of the kitchen.

ONDREJ wasn't quite sure what had just happened. He'd come into the kitchen to find something to eat. He hadn't meant to pick a fight, but when he'd seen Archie there, staring so forlornly at his dinner, something inside Ondrej had broken. He'd been missing his nights spent with Archie, missed the easy rapport they'd developed lately. Now he felt like he'd been left. But they still lived in the same house.

It was up there with his worst nightmares. Would Archie kick him out now?

And what the hell had he even done to earn all this hostility from Archie?

Ondrej leaned against the counter and pressed a hand to his forehead. He turned over every conversation he and Archie'd had in the past few days. When had Archie changed? What had gone wrong?

Ondrej had spoken out of turn, hadn't he? He'd called the relationship a fraud at the end of the meeting with Nancy Smalls. But he'd meant that in the past tense. Hadn't he? Because he'd thought things were changing between them, but maybe that wasn't what Archie wanted.

And when Archie had started putting distance between them, and he said that thing about how Ondrej could get a work visa and end the whole charade, well, Ondrej's first thought had been that Archie only seemed so desperate for Ondrej to stay because he needed the money. And so Ondrej could stay, if he kept to his own room and they lived like neighbors instead of lovers or husbands. The very thought made Ondrej's veins feel like they were filled with ice water.

He opened and closed the refrigerator a few times without deciding what he wanted to eat. He could make something, he could heat up leftovers, or he could even have something delivered.

There were too many options.

He leaned forward and pressed his forehead to the freezer door. What did Archie want? Why was he upset? Did he want Ondrej to stay or go?

And why did Ondrej care so much?

Well, that last question had an obvious answer.

Ondrej made sure the refrigerator was shut and then walked down to the office. The door was closed. Ondrej spent a moment imaging Archie hunched over his desk, shoveling food in his mouth while he stared at spreadsheets and plans on his laptop. Ondrej wondered how many nights Archie had spent just like that before Ondrej had moved in. Probably quite a few.

Archie didn't get out much, did he? Probably he'd been working like a crazy man since his father's death, trying valiantly to save his company. And Ondrej was a part of that solution, but he also knew, deep down, that it wasn't about the money anymore. Otherwise Archie wouldn't have reacted so drastically to the mere suggestion it might be.

Ondrej knocked softly on the door. "I know you said you wanted to be alone," he said, "but can I please come in? I want to talk to you."

He heard shuffling on the other side of the door. It opened a crack and Archie looked out. "What?"

"I'm sorry if I've offended you somehow, or if you're upset. I'd like to make it up to you."

Archie sighed. "It's not you. You didn't really do anything. It's me and my... well."

"I do care about you, Archie. That's not a lie."

"I know, but... I can't really explain it. And I've... I've had a rough day. I just want some time to myself."

"Okay."

"So please, can you just leave me alone for a little while?"

"Fine, just... before you put yourself in a funk, I think you've misunderstood some of the things that I've said, and I wanted to clarify—"

"No, don't bother. It's all a fraud. All of it. Our relationship, me, all of it. So can I just have a few goddamn minutes to wallow in how completely awful I feel? Please?"

The thought that if Archie was really in such a dark place, he might do something stupid, passed through Ondrej's head. "You won't—"

"I'm just going to eat my dinner and go to bed. All right?"

So Ondrej left him. He ordered dinner from the local Italian place, including a big slice of tiramisu, Archie's favorite. He put a sticky note on top of the plastic container, on which he wrote, *Peace Offering*. He left the box outside the office, which Archie had yet to leave.

It wasn't about the money. None of this was about money anymore. Ondrej was falling for Archie, and he knew Archie had fallen for him, but instead of being together, they were stuck in some kind of standoff while they worked out how they really felt.

As Ondrej headed down to the den to watch TV for a bit—hoping for a distraction from Archie's mood—he heard Archie walk in through the kitchen's other door and run water over his dishes. So at least he wasn't doing himself too much harm while stuck in his funk.

After an hour of the TV not successfully distracting him, Ondrej gave up and went up the stairs. He stopped in his bedroom first, where he stripped off his clothes, tossed them in the hamper, and then pulled on a pair of flannel pajama pants. He looked at the bed, still made from Hildy's most recent visit, but the prospect of going to bed alone again made him sad. So instead he padded down the hall to Archie's room. The door was closed—a rarity, given that the door had been open more often than not for weeks—but Ondrej pushed inside anyway.

He was worried now. Probably it was irrational to assume Archie would do something to harm himself, but Ondrej didn't know how bad a mood like this could get. This lack of knowledge was probably a problem, but it was something he'd address later.

As he slipped through the door, Ondrej realized there was a reason he was pursuing this so hard. If he didn't care about Archie, he wouldn't be bothering to try to make Archie feel better. He wouldn't be sneaking into Archie's room at night to make sure he was okay. No, Ondrej needed Archie, just as surely as Archie needed Ondrej, and Ondrej knew he had to find a way to break through Archie's icy exterior.

Archie was asleep, or appeared to be. He was curled up fetal on his side of the bed, the covers pulled up to his chin. Ondrej slid under the covers and spooned up behind him.

Archie made a noise, kind of a squeaky murmur, so Ondrej put his arm around him.

"Ondrej, I can't…."

So he'd been awake after all. Ondrej kissed his shoulder. "Shh." Then, considering, he said, "Remember the night I told my mother I'd married you?"

Archie let out a breath. "Yes."

"This is like that. You're upset and I'm trying to make you feel better."

"I'm upset about you."

Spoken so plainly, the sentiment went straight to Ondrej's heart. "I know. But just... I don't know exactly what has you upset, but I want to make it better. And I didn't want to go to bed alone."

Archie pressed back against Ondrej. "All right."

"Good."

"Thank you for the tiramisu."

"Of course."

IT was hard to deny that Archie slept more soundly when Ondrej was in bed with him. But it wasn't something he could get used to, because as he got out of bed the next morning, he didn't really feel better.

Oh, he appreciated that Ondrej had left him some dessert, and that he'd crawled into bed, and he believed that Ondrej thought he was being sincere. On the other hand, Archie couldn't quite believe in their relationship. It felt too fragile, too precarious, and Ondrej had more or less made it clear that they'd pass the time together, but Archie was certain he'd opt to leave once he got his green card. Or if he managed to procure a work visa. Whichever came first.

Archie couldn't deal with it if Ondrej left.

That was the real issue. He wasn't willing to get in any further, wasn't willing to get his heart stomped on any more than it already had been.

Ondrej didn't stir until Archie was already mostly dressed. Archie was tying his tie when Ondrej sat up, his hair askew.

"You leaving?" Ondrej asked.

"Yeah, I have to go into the office." Obviously. It was Friday.

Ondrej nodded. "Listen, about last night—"

"Can we not?" Archie didn't want to drag this out any more.

"I just wanted to apologize for—"

"I heard you the first time. I accept your apology. But I think it's probably better if we stay apart for a while."

"Why?"

"I know you mean well." Archie slid his suit jacket on over his shoulders. "But at the end of the day, we've still committed a fraud, and even if we get over that, I don't know. It seems like too shaky a foundation for a relationship. I can't seem to let go of the idea that what we have is fake and will always be."

"Even after all that's happened between us?"

"And," Archie added as he checked his appearance in the mirror, "I don't have it in me to have sex with you to pass the time until you get your green card and leave me. I just can't. I thought maybe I could, but I know now that's not true. So I really think it's better for us to just go back to our separate bedrooms. All right? We can be roommates, can't we?"

Ondrej's eyes were wide. But he nodded slowly. "If that's what you want."

"It is."

"All right, Archie."

Archie nodded. That wasn't as satisfying as he'd thought it would be. Ondrej's persistence the previous night had pissed him off, actually, and he'd thought stating clearly how he felt would put Ondrej in his place.

Instead, Archie felt empty.

But, figuring he couldn't do any more damage that morning, he smoothed his hand down the front of his tie one more time.

"I'll see you later, Ondrej."

"Yeah." Ondrej looked dazed.

Not willing to linger, Archie left.

Chapter Seventeen

IT wasn't a fraud. Not anymore. It wasn't fake. Ondrej paced the den, trying to work out his own feelings and how he could apologize to Archie. He knew this situation had stopped being just a façade the night of the gala. But then, what was it now? And what did Ondrej want?

He was coming around to the idea that what he wanted was Archie.

He sat in the den, mostly staring at the blank TV, trying to work out the best course of action.

Four months in New York City, and all he had to show for it was a sham marriage and a crumbling mansion. But he could make a good life for himself here. He could find his purpose—be it at Katsaros Holdings or somewhere else—and he could build a life with Archie. With an Archie who had agreed to take down the mask of his public persona when he was home and in a private space.

Because Amy was right: Archie was a marshmallow. He put on the gruff, somewhat abrasive mask for his employees and the jovial, charming mask for his wealthy peers, but those weren't him. He genuinely cared about people, for one thing, and he had a certain amount of natural charm. Ondrej was getting better at differentiating the real man from the public image, and he was very much starting to care for the real man. Ondrej could see himself spending time with the actual Archie for the foreseeable future, and not just as a means to an end.

For the first time, Ondrej let himself really consider the possibilities. He'd had a handful of short-term relationships and one long-term relationship in his twenties, but none of them had gotten to the phase where he'd really contemplated the future. And he realized he'd always pictured a life of love and success and possibly also children and family. It had taken getting out of Prague to see that his parents' shortsighted ways were not the only ways, and now he had many opportunities at his fingertips, including a good man who'd likely make an excellent husband and father.

A toasted marshmallow of a man Ondrej was coming to care for a great deal.

Which is why it destroyed him to think he'd upset Archie.

Archie had made his feelings clear. That Archie had feelings for Ondrej was both terrifying and exhilarating. Ondrej wanted to do right by Archie, but he knew the stakes were higher now.

It wasn't about the company, not anymore. It wasn't even about Ondrej staying in the States or Archie getting enough money to keep his company afloat. It was about figuring out how two people who had been thrown together for convenience could be with each other for real, for many years to come.

Hildy came into the den, wheeling the vacuum cleaner. She surveyed the floors and then moved over to the rug in front of the sofa. "You're tracking in dust from the hallway. Look at the footprints!"

Ondrej had been wearing dark socks and hadn't noticed the dust. "So sorry," he said, dusting the bottoms of his feet off with his hands.

"You're dressed up. Why aren't you at the office?"

He'd gotten dressed a few hours before and thought about going to the office and arguing on his own behalf, but he figured at this point that would be too much. Archie had made his feelings clear, and he'd stated he wanted some distance from Ondrej. So Ondrej would accede to his wishes. "Archie needed to work. He asked me to leave him alone for a while."

Hildy shook her head. "That boy is so lonely."

Ondrej wasn't sure what that had to do with anything. "No, that's not…. He told me he wanted some time apart. We had kind of a big argument last night."

Hildy clucked her tongue. "That man. He's spent his whole life trying to be what his father wants but never took the time to figure out what *he* wants. So now he runs that company by himself and works too much. I thought you moving in would help, but he seems the same."

Ondrej balked. "You don't even know what the argument was about."

"I don't need to know. I've known Archie for a long time." She shrugged. "So you had a fight. Archie assumed it was a bigger deal than it actually was, shut you out, and went to spend the day in his office. Is that about the sum of it?"

Hildy was surprisingly astute. Ondrej made a mental note to give her a raise. "It was a pretty big deal. We argued about some things fundamental to our relationship."

Hildy waved her hand. "Sure you did. My husband and I, we start fighting about what we want to watch on TV, and soon we're fighting about how he thinks I'm too indulgent with the kids. My oldest just left for college, you know. I try to call him a few times a week. Too much, says my husband. Then we're debating parenting philosophy, and it feels like a lot." She shook her head. "Fights happen. Some of them are petty, some of them are about big issues. The key to staying married is to talk these things out. Find common ground. Don't walk away and don't let hurt feelings fester."

Ondrej tried to digest that, both the fact that the housekeeper was giving him marriage advice and that her advice was excellent. "Should I have pushed harder? Even though he made it clear he doesn't want me to?"

Hildy shrugged. "You're good for him, you know. He seems happier lately. Less lonely. But even with you here, he locks himself in that office downtown."

It surprised Ondrej that Archie had spoken to Hildy recently enough for her to have picked up on a change in his mood, but then he remembered she'd come in first thing that morning and Archie had given her a cup of coffee and a bagel.

Because Archie was not the charming tyrant his father had been, but instead was the sort of man who made sure everyone around him got enough to eat; he was trying to save a company without laying anyone off because he couldn't bear the thought of someone in his employ losing his or her job.

"Archie is a good man," Ondrej said.

"The best. Don't let the nonsense they print on the society pages tell you otherwise."

Ondrej laughed because the comment so surprised him. "You read the society pages?"

"Of course. Who doesn't?"

Hildy started vacuuming the rug, so Ondrej left the room and walked into the foyer to put his shoes away.

Archie didn't know what he wanted out of life, she had said. But Archie wanted Ondrej. The rest of it, Ondrej didn't know about, but he could give Archie at least one thing.

So he formed a plan. Because he knew Archie was too far in his own head to take anything Ondrej said at face value. Ondrej would have to prove himself.

All this effort for a man Ondrej wasn't even sure he'd liked a few weeks ago. But clearly something had changed, and Ondrej was determined to explore it.

Chapter Eighteen

WHEN Archie came home, the overhead lights in the foyer were out, but a long line of candles led toward the formal dining room in the western wing of the house. Ondrej must have put them there, but what on earth was going on?

Curious, Archie followed the candles.

Archie used the formal dining room even less than the living room—he much preferred eating at the more casual table in the kitchen—but its ostentatious elegance was dimmed by low lighting. A huge flower arrangement sat at the center of the dining table, and long, thin taper candles circled the flowers. It was beautiful and, well, romantic.

Ondrej stood at one end of the table with a smile on his face.

"What's all this?" Archie asked.

"A romantic gesture."

Archie didn't believe it. He shook his head. He didn't have the energy to put on a show tonight, for whoever's benefit, and he couldn't figure out why Ondrej had gone to these lengths inside the house, which was mostly a sanctuary from all the lies. "Ondrej, I appreciate the lengths you went to, but I can't—"

"I think you misunderstand me." Ondrej walked around the table toward Archie. "I've been thinking about us all day. Here's what I've concluded. This relationship started out as a convenient arrangement, but the more we get to know each other, the more we like each other, right?"

Archie held his breath but nodded.

"When you asked me after the immigration interview what I thought, I answered that our relationship was built on a fraud. We'd kept up the farce for Ms. Smalls, but the truth is that this stopped being a farce for me some time ago. I do genuinely like you, Archie, the more I get to know you. I seriously misjudged you when we met, and I want to make up for that. I want to prove to you that I'm being genuine and that this is not an act. So I've decided we need to do something romantic."

Archie was reluctant. He liked what he heard, but this could still be a recipe for getting hurt in the long run. He opened his mouth but couldn't think of what to say.

"I haven't convinced you," said Ondrej. "So consider this. We live in strange, modern times. Can you imagine how many gay men married women in order to get green cards in the last one hundred years? To get away from oppressive regimes in their home countries? My mother doesn't approve of me, but my life wouldn't be in danger if I were to go back to Prague. I don't want to go back, but I had some options. I didn't have to marry a woman. Instead, I married a man who I'm attracted to and have come to care about. No, we didn't know each other well on our wedding day, but that has changed in the last few weeks, wouldn't you say?"

Archie agreed, but he still couldn't do much more than nod.

"I believe I understand you now, Archie. You project this image of a tough businessman, someone who is single-minded and doesn't take shit from anyone. You run your company the way your father did, or the way you think he would have wanted. But inside, you're a marshmallow."

Archie balked.

"I'm serious," Ondrej said, stepping closer. "You're kindhearted and soft. I don't mean that as an insult. To me, that makes you more appealing. You have real compassion for the people who work for you—for other people in general. It makes you different from your father, but in the best way. I like this Archie." Inches away now, Ondrej pointed at Archie's chest, his finger grazing Archie's tie. "I like this man much more than the man you tried to make me think you were when we just met."

Archie found that difficult to believe. Marshmallows were sweet and soft. Archie tried to portray himself as hard, but he knew he was too sensitive. He could hear his father's voice in his head whenever he tried to figure out how to save employees from pink slips. He was weak. He was a sissy.

But Ondrej was standing right here. "I like the man you really are. And I'd like to take that man on a proper date. No strategizing about how to fool the public.

No business talk. Just you and me and a nice dinner. Then after, there's a jazz ensemble playing at a club I know, and I thought it might be nice to hear some real American music. With you. What do you say?"

It was a hard offer to turn down, but Archie still hesitated. He wasn't sure why; Ondrej seemed sincere. But he had a niggling feeling that this was all flimsy and temporary, that a year from now, or two, whenever Ondrej's green card came through, this would end.

Ondrej stepped closer, within Archie's personal space. He put his hands on Archie's waist. "I'm being completely sincere. I know you have doubts, that you doubt *me*, but I want this, and I think you do too. Maybe you don't believe me. So I'll prove it to you."

Ondrej leaned forward and kissed Archie.

And Archie was lost. He couldn't hold out any longer. He wanted this too much. He put his hands on the sides of Ondrej's face to hold him there while they explored each other's mouths. How he'd been holding Ondrej away, Archie didn't know, but he didn't want to any longer.

Ondrej pulled away slowly and smiled at Archie. "So will you go out with me tonight?"

"Well, when you put it like that...."

ONDREJ had called Amy for restaurant recommendations, and she'd given him the name of what she called a "new American" restaurant that she ate at with her husband all the time. She assured Ondrej the food was good and the atmosphere was romantic.

It was a nice night, so Ondrej proposed walking across town. He knew the fastest route from one side of Central Park to the other—he'd needed something to do when he wasn't working—though he wasn't opposed to a more meandering walk. It was a nice night, warm but not too hot. Archie seemed game as they crossed Fifth Avenue to the park entrance.

The big kiss notwithstanding, Archie still seemed reluctant, walking a foot or more away from Ondrej as they made their way through the park. In the spirit of keeping his promise, Ondrej spoke just to make conversation. "I'd seen photos of Central Park before I moved here, but I don't think I ever appreciated how big it is until I tried to get across it."

"My nanny used to bring me to the playground we just passed," said Archie. "Her name was Sonia. She lives in the Bronx now. We still talk sometimes and exchange Christmas cards." Archie kicked a rock. "I was closer to her than my mother in some ways. Mother was never home. She was always busy with some function or other."

"I was raised by nannies too," said Ondrej. "The house was run by Ada, sort of the head housekeeper, and she watched me most days. Then they hired a tutor named Doubravka who taught me grammar and math, mostly, and also helped with my English. She had an American boyfriend, whom I thought was the coolest. He was my first crush."

"It's funny, sometimes I feel like there really might be an ocean between us, but I suppose we do have a lot in common."

"Or it's a reversal." Ondrej gestured toward a turn in the path, and Archie followed. Ondrej said, "My family spent more time in the eighties pretending to be wealthy than actually being wealthy. The upper-class families in Prague put on a lot of airs while their bank accounts drained. But government policy effectively wrecked the economy by preventing any real innovation. It's really only because of my grandparents that my family had anything."

"Your parents wouldn't move?"

"No. My father's family had been in power in Prague since it was part of Bohemia. Like your mother, I would think."

"Minus a few hundred years, yes."

Ondrej chuckled. "Well, he felt strongly connected to the city. And my mother wouldn't leave without my father. So we stayed."

"But you left."

"Yes, well. There are only so many times you can hear about how you're shaming the family legacy by living off inherited money and not getting married." Ondrej sighed. "I didn't love Prague, not the way my parents did. But within a week of being in New York, I knew this was where I belonged."

"For what it's worth, I am glad you're here. It's not exaggerating to say my life has changed irrevocably in the last few weeks."

"Mine too." Whether the change was for the better remained to be seen.

They arrived at the restaurant a short time later and were shown to a table off to the side, ideal more for talking than for being seen, which was how Ondrej had planned it. The restaurant was dimly lit and romantic, with candles flickering on each table. It was perfect, in other words.

After a waiter served their wine, Archie said, "What about America has surprised you most so far?"

Ondrej smiled, enjoying the amused expression on Archie's face. It made him look boyish and curious. "I'd heard from friends more worldly than I that America was very repressed and conservative. But New York is more free than I expected. Everyone just goes about their business."

"That's New York. Things are different in the rest of the country."

"I know. It just wasn't what I expected. Well, a lot of things didn't turn out how I expected. I certainly didn't expect to get married. But I didn't expect to want to stay this bad, either."

"I've never lived anywhere else. I can't imagine moving."

"You didn't grow up in a communist country, I suppose."

"True, but you know there's something magic here. Something magic about New York. You can't imagine leaving, can you?"

Ondrej smiled at that. "You're right. I certainly don't want to."

They spent the next forty minutes discussing lighter topics: Ondrej's favorite American movie (*Dirty Dancing*) and Archie's (*Wayne's World*); books they'd read that summer, or that Ondrej had read, since Archie rarely had time to finish a book; tabloid gossip; the relative merits of Ondrej's new cell phone; Archie's favorite fashion designers; TV shows Archie wished he had time to see but that Ondrej had binged on and could recommend; and even a little office gossip. Archie seemed especially tickled that one of his best marketing guys was dating a woman from accounts payable.

"I guess if I keep them in the office all the time, it's only fair that they date each other," Archie said, chuckling.

Ondrej laughed too, but he said, "I don't know whether that's a good thing or not. This American work ethic…."

"I know. I was kidding."

The long hours some of the employees had to work was a topic worth pursuing, but not now. Ondrej smiled at Archie but made a mental note to bring it up later. This time was for themselves, not for work or the company.

As they worked their way through the chef's tasting menu, discussion turned toward the food. Archie didn't care for the duck liver mousse, though Ondrej thought it delicious. They agreed the asparagus dish was tasty in unexpected ways. They each tried the elk; Archie ruled it too gamey, and Ondrej didn't quite like it either, but he couldn't put his finger on why. He wondered if he perhaps just did not have the English vocabulary to articulate to Archie what he liked and didn't. There was a potato dish that was divine, a pork belly dish that was savory and satisfying, and a duck breast that Archie thought typified "umami," whatever the hell that was. As a palate cleanser, a waiter brought them a cheese course—mostly sheep's milk cheeses, which Ondrej admitted he preferred to goat cheese.

Then, finally, dessert. Ondrej expected something small and pretentious, as most of the meal had been, tasty though it was. But instead, they received a healthy slab of black-and-white mousse cake, with two forks to share.

"Perfect," said Archie.

Ondrej gamely took a bite. It was light and fluffy, and the sweetness was undercut by a bit of salt in the ganache on top. The cake was really good, in fact.

"This is a marvelous way to end a meal," Archie said, eating with gusto.

"We'll have to walk back just to burn off all these calories."

"Didn't you want to check out that jazz bar?"

Thus, a half hour later, they were ensconced in a corner booth behind a tiny round table. At Archie's insistence, they'd switched from the wine at the restaurant to cheap beer. He explained that made the experience more American.

"This beer tastes like piss," Ondrej commented.

"Authenticity!" said Archie.

So Ondrej laughed, because Archie was getting into it. Archie explained about a brief flirtation with playing the saxophone in high school—"Mother discouraged it because it wasn't piano or violin or a classier instrument, but that was part of the appeal for me," he said—and a resulting fascination with jazz. Ondrej could listen to Archie talk this enthusiastically about anything, so he basked in the trivia about Louis Armstrong and Miles Davis and Thelonious Monk.

Then the band came on, and it was like nothing Ondrej had ever heard before. The first few numbers seemed percussion-heavy and lacking a coherent melody, but Ondrej found himself bobbing his head along with the bass line. The music was expressive and beautiful in its way.

"Must be hard to dance to this," Ondrej said.

"I don't know that you're supposed to. Some older jazz, some of the standards, sure, but this modern jazz, less so."

Ondrej nodded, thinking about what a revelation it had been to dance with Archie. The band had played jazz at the charity gala too, but older jazz, less experimental, more melodic. The old songs were meant to be danced to, but this was something else entirely.

Archie seemed to be really into this, and his enthusiasm was catching. Ondrej wanted to be a part of it, so he reached under the table and took Archie's hand. Archie smiled at him, and together, they listened to two more sets and drank more cheap beer.

They stumbled into a cab a while later—they were both a little drunk, and Archie insisted they skip the late-night walk across the park—and arrived home around midnight. Ondrej thought he'd accomplished his mission. Archie was smiling.

"Come to bed with me tonight," Archie said.

It was what Ondrej wanted to hear, but after days of Archie putting him off, it felt strange. "Are you sure?"

Archie nodded. "I'm sure. I know I've been rude—"

"You were protecting your heart," Ondrej said.

Archie's face melted into a soft smile. "Yes."

"And I'm telling you with my actions tonight that you don't need to protect yourself from me anymore. I want what you want."

Archie hesitated. "I'm not sure that—"

"Archie. Trust me. Okay? I want to be with you. For the foreseeable future. Not because we're married and not because I need the green card, but because I like you. I like us together. That's what I want."

Archie bit his lip and nodded. The gesture was endearing, boyish again in its way. Ondrej walked closer and kissed Archie softly. "Trust me," Ondrej repeated.

"I do," whispered Archie.

Ondrej followed Archie up the stairs. He wanted Archie, not just because he'd been deprived of sex for the past few nights or because he was aroused, but because he just wanted to be with Archie, end of story. Tonight had been more about getting to know each other than a prelude to sex. Ondrej wanted to spend more time with Archie, wanted to get closer to him, and yes, wanted to make love.

For the foreseeable future.

And wasn't that a kick in the head? Ondrej was falling in love with his own husband.

Chapter Nineteen

ARCHIE held Ondrej in his arms as Ondrej straddled him, grinding against him and kissing his lips softly. They were both naked, giving Archie access to all of Ondrej's beautiful skin, which he stroked reverently wherever he could reach.

Ondrej dipped his head and kissed Archie, sinking his teeth into Archie's lower lip. Archie groaned and thrust up against him.

Warmth spread across Archie's chest, and it wasn't just the pending orgasm building. Archie was coming to really cherish the man in his arms. There was no fraud here, no pretense, nothing but two men bared to each other, sharing a perfect moment.

Archie's tiny bedside lamp was the only real light source aside from the orange haze from streetlights filtering in through the gauzy curtains. It had the effect of making Ondrej's skin glow. Archie wanted to taste that, so he pressed kisses to Ondrej's chest, to his collarbone. He bit Ondrej's nipple, which made him gasp and groan and thrust his fingers into Archie's hair.

"Fuck, I'm close," Ondrej said.

Archie still wanted to ask if Ondrej desired him for anything more than sex and a green card, not completely convinced despite Ondrej's speech downstairs, but that would break the moment. Ondrej slid up and down Archie's cock, and the feeling was so exquisite Archie's mind went blank for a moment, but he couldn't shake the doubt. The date tonight should have convinced him they had a future, and Archie believed Ondrej when he said he wanted to have a relationship with Archie, but... the doubt still hung there, a hovering blackness in the back of his mind.

But Ondrej squeezed Archie's cock and rode him for all he was worth.

Archie was falling for Ondrej in a way that felt beautiful and deep and unlike anything Archie had ever experienced before—and if Ondrej didn't return those feelings, Archie wasn't sure what he'd do.

For now, he was determined to savor it.

He pushed Ondrej off him and rolled Ondrej onto his side. Ondrej groaned and stretched out his long body. He said, "I need you, Archie."

Ondrej had a tattoo on his left side, a black vine with little flowers that wound its way up from his hip to his armpit. It was striking against his olive skin. Archie slid his tongue along it, pressed his lips to it, and fanned his fingers across Ondrej's back and belly. Ondrej murmured appreciatively.

"You're so beautiful," Archie said, pressing Ondrej onto his back. He hovered over Ondrej and kissed him soundly as Ondrej lifted his legs. Archie slid back home, inside Ondrej, into his arms.

"Archie, I...."

Archie looked down and met Ondrej's gaze. They stared at each other for a long moment. Ondrej had little gold flecks in his eyes Archie hadn't noticed before, had a soft dusting of freckles across his nose that was only really noticeable when he blushed, had a look on his face that he was holding on by the tips of his fingers.

Archie kept thrusting his hips, the friction pulling something from his body, spurring him forward. Everything in his body was screaming, waiting for that release, rushing for it.

But he had to know what Ondrej was about to say.

He missed the opportunity, though. Ondrej moaned, "Archie," and then he dug his nails into the skin of Archie's shoulder blades. He threw his head back and cried out and came all over his belly.

Archie's whole world went blank, the pleasure white hot as he emptied into Ondrej, and he clutched at Ondrej as he groaned and came.

He buried his face in the crook of Ondrej's neck as things around them settled, and he regretted a little that it had happened so fast, that he couldn't have drawn out what Ondrej was about to say, because it felt important.

"Amazing," Ondrej murmured, petting Archie's hair.

And because it was, Archie kept his mouth shut and snuggled against Ondrej's skin.

SOMETHING still felt off about Archie, like he was still holding back, but it was hard to put a finger on what could be going on given that they'd just made passionate, sweaty love and the man in question was currently holding on to Ondrej as if he were afraid Ondrej would float away.

Ondrej was thirsty, but he didn't dare get up.

The sex had been amazing, but Ondrej felt more than just sated. It wasn't even that Ondrej wanted to date Archie, though he did; marriage aside, they'd be doing more than just dating. Ondrej had no way to describe or quantify this, however. He felt the emotion and intimacy between them, yes. But he felt more too.

Ondrej shifted, pressing his back into Archie's front. The texture of Archie, his chest hair and smooth skin, tickled Ondrej's shoulders, but Ondrej wanted that tickle, wanted to feel Archie pressed against him. Archie murmured and tightened his grasp, as if that were possible, wrapping his arms fully around Ondrej and murmuring nonsense into Ondrej's shoulder. "Beautiful," Archie said, over and over again.

Ondrej sighed and sank into it, savored it, wondered if it would always feel this good.

He wanted to say something, but he didn't know how to say it.

"I want you to know," Archie said, saving Ondrej from filling the silence, "I don't take this lightly."

"What do you mean?" Ondrej asked, though he knew.

"Tonight you did something romantic, and the evening was perfect. That's important. Right now, this?" Archie squeezed Ondrej again. "This feels important. I want to think it's not fleeting or temporary."

"It's not."

Archie took a deep breath, and it rattled against Ondrej's hair. "Cards on the table, okay?"

Sensing Archie was going to say something he wouldn't like, Ondrej wriggled out of Archie's grasp and turned around. He settled back into the bed and put a hand on Archie's hip to show he wasn't leaving, just that he wanted to see Archie's face. "What is it?"

"You wanted honesty, so here it is. I've been attracted to you since the moment I set eyes on you. That first moment I saw you, I thought that really was it for me. I wanted to get to know you. The whole reason I went along with this whole proposal at all was that I thought you were gorgeous. I mean, Marketa helped quite a bit, played us both like violins, I think, but I went along with it because I thought there might be a chance we'd end up like this."

Ondrej let that wash over him. Not wanting to surrender completely just yet, he said, "That's a hell of a lot of trouble to go to just to get laid."

Archie laughed and rubbed his forehead with the heel of his hand as he rolled onto his back. "I know. It's so stupid. I mean, I needed the money too, obviously. But I hoped from the moment you consented to the marriage that maybe something could happen with us. If I'm honest, though, I thought it would be just sex, and that would have been all right because I don't get to go to bed with men who look like you very often."

Ondrej propped his head up on one elbow. "Just sex? Because I thought that wasn't all you wanted."

Archie rolled his eyes. "Ugh, I'm going about this all wrong. What I'm trying to say is that for weeks now— months, maybe—I've been wanting to go to bed with you, and ever since you moved into the house, I had this hope that you'd want that too. That's how it started. You didn't seem into it, though, so I sort of resigned myself to that not being the outcome of this. Which was okay, you know, I could handle being your friend and helping you out until you got your green card. It would be like sitting in the room with a chocolate cake and being told you can't have any, but I could have done it."

Everything was swimming in Ondrej. Unable to formulate a response or even interpret exactly what the point of this was, he blurted, "But instead we fucked."

Archie barked out a surprised laugh. "Yeah. We fucked. A lot. But I'm failing horribly to explain that the sex is beside the point because I really like you a lot, more than I even expected to, and what I've discovered over the last couple of weeks is that I like being with you. It's not just sex. There's a real bond between us, or at least I think there is. That's why I was so reluctant to take this further. And so being with you is better than what I pictured, and I want us to keep being together. My heart soared tonight when you made your romantic gesture. Goddamn soared. But there's still a part of me that doesn't believe it, which I think is my defense mechanism against getting my heart completely destroyed. Because if all this is still just a joke to you—"

"It's not." No hesitation. Ondrej was in this just as surely as Archie was.

"I couldn't take you breaking my heart and then leaving me. Not yet, anyway."

"You still think I will?"

"You think you'll stay?"

"I want to." But even Ondrej had to admit that as hard as he was falling for Archie, the future still felt uncertain. He didn't know how the rest of the week would go, didn't know how the rest of the month or year would go. He didn't know if this was just short-lived, sex-fueled euphoria or real emotion making him feel so close to Archie.

"Cards on the table," Ondrej said.

"Yeah." Archie looked away.

"I started thinking about you as a way to pass the time. Like, we might as well fuck because we're attracted to each other and we're stuck with each other for however long the CIS stalls with my green card application."

"Oh."

Ondrej reached over and slid his fingers under Archie's chin, pushing gently until Archie faced him and their gazes met. Ondrej continued, "But this stopped being about just the green card quite some time ago, I think. You were right: I probably could have gotten a work visa if I'd given it more time, and spared us both a lot of drama and paperwork. But that's not what this is about anymore. The whole reason for the romantic gesture tonight was to prove I have real feelings for you and I want to explore them." He took a deep breath. "I think we hesitate now because we don't know what the future holds, and maybe a year from now we'll hate each other, but for now, let's pretend that's not the case. Let's be together. For real."

Archie sighed and nodded. "We are already married."

Ondrej couldn't help but smile. "So we did this backwards. We'll end up in the right place eventually, don't you think?"

"I sincerely hope so."

Not liking the sadness in Archie's expression, Ondrej leaned over to kiss him. Archie tilted his head and deepened the kiss, sliding his tongue into Ondrej's mouth. Archie had been right: this did feel important. The tingling spreading through Ondrej's body wasn't just arousal, it was excitement at being with this particular man. Because Archie was exciting to be with. This thing between them made Ondrej happy.

"I want to make you happy, Archie," Ondrej said, realizing that Archie had probably long been as lonely as he was, trapped in this world of artifice without any room to be himself. Ondrej at least had the escape hatch of leaving his home and coming here, to New York, where he had plenty of space. Archie didn't have the same luxury.

"That may not be possible," Archie said, "but I'm willing to let you try."

"Good." Ondrej kissed Archie again. "You're not alone anymore."

Archie balked. "How did you—"

"Shh," Ondrej said, kissing Archie again, no longer wanting to talk.

ARCHIE lay awake for a long time after Ondrej fell asleep.

He turned over what Ondrej had said. You're not alone anymore. You don't have to be alone.

That Ondrej had clued in to the loneliness Archie never let himself acknowledge probably said something about how close they were growing.

He'd meant what he'd said; he'd been hoping for sex and wound up in a relationship with a man he really liked. This was far beyond what he'd expected. And he had been holding out hope that they had a future together despite the piece of paper legally binding them, because he couldn't count on this, not yet. Not until he felt like he could trust that Ondrej wouldn't leave once the green card came through. He believed Ondrej now, believed he meant what he said, but there was still too much uncertainty for Archie to properly invest his heart in this project.

But if tonight was a taste of what could be....

Ondrej snored softly. There was intimacy in that too, him just snoozing comfortably in bed beside Archie. Archie reached over and lightly traced his fingers along Ondrej's arm. Ondrej stirred but didn't wake up. Archie pulled his hand away and closed his eyes.

Could they do this? Could they be together as a real couple, or had they spent too much time together perpetrating a fraud? Was pretending everything was okay too much of a habit for Archie to break? And would everything fall apart if Archie tapped into what he was really feeling?

He didn't know, and he didn't like the uncertainty. Everything was uncertain, from whether his company would make payroll in three months to his future with Ondrej, and he was going crazy from not knowing how things would turn out.

But if what Ondrej said was true, if Archie had a real partner and didn't have to be alone anymore, maybe things would be all right. If the company fell apart but Archie still had Ondrej, he'd survive.

Archie took a few deep breaths and tried to believe that he could have a real partner to help him through the uncertain future. With Ondrej at his side, the mess at Katsaros Holdings felt less daunting.

And with that thought, Archie drifted off to sleep.

Chapter Twenty

READING through manager's reports was not the most stimulating way to spend an afternoon, but Ondrej had to give Archie some credit for trying to make it fun. They'd taken over a conference room so that they could spread out on the table. Archie had made a fresh pot of coffee and ordered in a bunch of junk food, which Marketa had dutifully delivered an hour before. Ondrej ate a handful of M&M's as he wrote another name on the list.

"It's hard not to feel like a judge sending a man to the gallows," Archie said.

"It's nothing nearly so dramatic. We're letting go employees who aren't serving you well. Hell, listen to this." Ondrej brandished the report. "This is about one of the guys in advertising. 'Joe is consistently a half hour or an hour late, despite being told repeatedly that his day is to start promptly at 9:00 a.m. He often leaves early as well. When actually in the office, he's slow, taking two or three times the amount of time to complete a project as everyone else in the department.' This is a salaried employee, so his slacking off costs you money. The manager has been wanting to lay him off for a while but didn't think he had the authority. He does say at the bottom of the report that this Joe does so little work, what he does do can be easily parceled out to the other people in the department."

"So I should lay him off."

"Yes. Well, that guy should be fired. But I've got about a dozen people on this list that we could lay off. Simply eliminating their salaries alone puts almost a million dollars per year back in your coffers. That's not to mention subsidizing their benefits packages."

"Right." Archie nodded slowly.

"Look, the best way to save money is through efficiency. That means cutting dead weight. You lay off employees who aren't earning their salaries, eliminate departments that don't do anything, trim wasteful spending. I know you really want this stadium project, but you frankly can't afford it unless you make some changes."

Archie just nodded.

"You're not actually sentencing anyone to death," Ondrej said. "These people have solid work experience at a well-regarded company they can use to prop up their résumé. The economy in this city has turned around in the last couple of years. These people will find jobs. And if they don't, they'll learn that slacking off has consequences and they'll shape up."

"That's harsh."

"It's realistic."

Archie sighed. "You really think we'll be able to stave off Dan? He still wants to sell off a large chunk of my assets. If the board sides with him, I'm through."

"I know. Dan complicates matters. It means the board has to find your proposal more persuasive. I'm convinced after the meeting that generally the board is on your side and wants to keep Katsaros together. Dan's hoping for a fat payout from Cochrane for your property so he can retire and move to the beach or whatever he's angling for. But if you can show that cleaning up the inefficiencies here and selling a few properties would pay off in the long run, you'll convince the board."

Archie nodded and went back to reading reports.

So Ondrej spent the next half hour jotting down a plan to make Katsaros run more efficiently. He still thought the stadium project was a financial black hole, but he knew Archie's heart was set on it. So, once he had some semblance of a plan, he passed it to Archie and said, "With the caveat that you could easily undo all of this if any part of the stadium goes over budget, here's how I think you make the company run better."

It wasn't a very elaborate plan. Ondrej wanted to combine two departments, cut about fifteen people, and start getting stricter when approving expense reports and equipment requests. He was certain he'd find all kinds of wasteful requests if he went through the files down in accounts payable: reimbursed meals for employees who weren't actually conducting company business, expensive flights when a cheaper flight or train ride was available, upgrades paid for by the company, and probably thousands of dollars in pens, paper, and other office supplies that walked off with employees each day.

Archie spent a few minutes looking it over, which encouraged Ondrej to think he was taking it seriously.

"You know," Archie said, "I have an MBA from a prestigious business school and grew up working in these offices, but I think you have a better head for business than I do."

Ondrej barked out a laugh, surprised by the compliment. "No."

"I'm serious. Or you're braver. I haven't wanted to change anything, but you're totally correct that there's all kinds of inefficiency in this company that could be cleaned up. Even just cracking down on what people are allowed to request reimbursements for could save me thousands of dollars."

"I'll be candid," Ondrej said. "I've talked to Amy and a few other managers, and the bottom line is that your employees were afraid of your father but didn't have much respect for him. The way you go tearing through the office sometimes, aping your father? That makes everyone think you're just the same. But you're not."

Archie bristled.

"I honestly mean that as a compliment." Ondrej paused to think about how best to phrase his thoughts. "Let me put it this way. If a well-regarded business consultant—not me, but someone with real credentials—recommended your father lay off twenty employees for the good of the company, would he even hesitate?"

Archie sighed. "No. Probably not. He was known for firing people on the spot if they so much as looked at him in a way he didn't like."

"Right. That's terror. You don't want your employees to be afraid of you. They won't want to work for you. The good ones will get fed up and find better jobs. You instead want to inspire people. You want to show you're talented. And I think even just sending the message that the guy who is only putting in six-hour days will get fired, but the guy who puts in extra hours gets rewarded with better projects and promotions is better. The employees will see that the slacker they resented because he was getting away with goofing off on company time is let go while their hard work is respected and rewarded."

Archie nodded. "You're right."

Ondrej was surprised he gave in so easily. He opted to press on. "I think a kinder, gentler approach will be more effective. Show the employees—hell, show the world—that you are not your father. You do business differently. You do business in a modern way. You, Archimedes Katsaros, do business better."

Archie hedged. He opened his mouth as if to speak a few times and then seemed to think better of it. Then he slumped in his chair. "Are you sure?"

"Yes. Absolutely. I know you loved your father and thought the world of him, which you should have. He was your father. But he's also the man who got the company into the mess you are currently trying to clean up. I don't know what caused it—if he made a few bad decisions or if he failed to adapt to the changing economy or if he didn't have enough oversight or even if he just was never as shrewd a businessman as he made people believe—but something went wrong somewhere along the line."

Archie nodded. His eyes were wide, and he stared unfocused at a spot on the table. "I know. I know all of that." He blinked a few times and looked at Ondrej. "But I keep falling into this trap where I'm not sure if my way is actually better. And I can't risk letting everything he built fall apart just because he made some bad choices toward the end of his life."

"So don't let it fall apart."

"Easy for you to say."

Ondrej reached over and took Archie's hand. He squeezed it gently. "I'll help you. We'll work together to solve this."

Archie frowned but then met Ondrej's gaze. "You're sure you want to?"

"We're a team, whether you like it or not. You gave me an office, remember? You told me you thought I had good business sense. So let me use it." Ondrej smiled. "Let's face it. Me sitting at home was doing no one any good. I just felt bored and listless. This will at least give me something to do all day. A purpose."

"I suppose so." But Archie didn't look convinced.

So Ondrej scooted closer and took Archie's other hand. "It also turns out I like working with you. If we keep this up, we might even make a good team. Here and at home."

Archie looked at their joined hands and then looked up at Ondrej. He took a deep breath. "Okay. We'll do it."

"Good."

Archie smiled slowly. "Should we shake on it? Sign a contract?"

"Yes, probably." Ondrej leaned forward. "But we can also seal it with a kiss."

The crease in Archie's brow finally faded. He smiled faintly and kissed Ondrej.

It was a relief, in a way, to have this, to be able to kiss and be affectionate with each other and have that affection be genuine instead of pretend. It was trite, his goofy line, but it made his heart beat at a giddy tempo.

Archie hummed, making Ondrej's lips vibrate, so he deepened the kiss, drawing Archie into it more.

Ondrej heard a squeak to his left and turned in time to see the accounting manager, Stephen, stumble through the door.

"Oh! I'm so sorry to interrupt."

Archie laughed and eased away from Ondrej. He winked before he turned to Stephen. "No need to apologize. We should have been working instead of making out. What do you need?"

"Marketa said you were in here. I just wanted to ask a few questions about the building on Eighty-Seventh Street. There are some discrepancies in the rental report, and I—"

"We were just wrapping up," Ondrej said.

"Yes," said Archie. "Let me just clean up here, and I'll meet you in my office in five minutes. All right?"

Stephen nodded and left.

Ondrej was almost glad they'd been caught; Stephen would likely mention walking in on the boss and his husband kissing each other in a conference room as an awkward story to someone else in the office, thus making it clear the relationship was real to the Katsaros employees. That lent some legitimacy to the relationship. They'd been caught, which only would have been possible if there was something to catch them doing.

Ondrej smiled to himself. Warmth spread through his chest as he gazed at his husband.

"I'll try your kinder, gentler approach because I agree it's probably a good idea," Archie said, gathering up the scattered reports. "But you do realize that most of the employees are going to credit you with softening me up."

Ondrej grinned. "I'm okay with that."

"Just so we're clear, it's not true."

"No, I know. You've always been a marshmallow."

Archie narrowed his eyes at Ondrej. Then he laughed, grabbed the stack of reports, and left the room.

LATER in the week, Archie passed a street vendor selling flowers as he walked home from the subway. He couldn't have said what struck him, but a particularly colorful bouquet of gerbera daisies caught his eye. He bought them and carried them home, intending to give them to Ondrej.

When he was about a block away from the house, he realized he didn't even know if Ondrej liked daisies. He'd bought flowers for Archie on the night of their big date, but did he like receiving flowers?

He didn't like these self-doubt stumbling blocks. They'd made so much progress in their relationship, and Archie felt like they had something real now, and he liked it, felt like it had real potential. This tangible thing they were building was far better than Archie's fondest imaginings of what married life would be like.

But it was hard to shake the feeling that it was all still a scam.

By the time Archie got to his front door, he'd decided that if Ondrej didn't like the flowers, he'd keep them himself. Maybe he'd put them in a vase in his office. That room could certainly use some color.

So resolved, he went inside.

When he called out for Ondrej, Ondrej popped his head into the foyer. "Oh, welcome home! Uh, don't be alarmed, but I've made a mess of the kitchen."

"Why?"

"Well, I was trying to cook. One of my grandmother's old recipes. I suppose I never quite mastered the art of not getting food everywhere when I cook. It seems to taste all right."

"I didn't know you cooked."

Ondrej smiled. "I have many hidden talents."

"If the meal is tasty, I'll help you clean after dinner."

"Deal." Ondrej turned to leave.

"Hey, wait!" Archie called.

"What? I have to check on the meal."

"I got you some flowers."

Archie braced himself for Ondrej's reaction. Flowers were always a dicey thing with male lovers. Some thought flowers were too feminine, some were fine with them, some were allergic, some just didn't like flowers.

But Ondrej's face seemed to melt. "Oh, Archie. They're lovely. Thank you."

Archie could do nothing but sigh happily.

Ondrej took the flowers and held the bouquet close to his chest before he turned on his heel and walked back toward the kitchen.

Archie followed, and when he got to the kitchen, Ondrej said, "Make yourself useful and find a vase."

Ondrej was right: he had made a mess of the kitchen. The sink was full of pots and bowls, there were smudges of who-only-knew-what on the counter, and something had been spilled on the stove. Ondrej held out the flowers for Archie to take back, so Archie took them and then pulled a tall glass vase out of one of the cabinets. He poured a little water in it and placed it on the table. Then he took the plastic wrapping off the flowers and propped them in the vase.

Ondrej pulled a casserole dish out of the oven and placed it on a trivet on the counter. Then he walked over to

Archie, slung an arm around him from behind, and rested his chin on Archie's shoulder. "They are really pretty," Ondrej said. "I appreciate the gesture. Thank you."

Archie rubbed Ondrej's arm, relieved that Ondrej liked them. "Thank you for dinner."

"Don't thank me yet. You haven't eaten it."

But Ondrej need not have worried. He'd made stuffed baked mushrooms served alongside potato dumplings and cabbage, accompanied by a light gravy. It was all delicious.

"We didn't always have meat available to us when I was a kid, so I got used to eating vegetarian. My grandmother, even after she moved to France, tended to like lighter fare anyway, nothing too rich or heavy. So that's what I learned to cook."

"It's really good," Archie said with his mouth full.

Ondrej laughed. "I'm glad you think so. Maybe next time I'll buy some meat and make some traditional Prague-style dishes. Goulash or beer sausage or something."

"I don't even know what goulash is."

Ondrej tsked. "Foolish American." He smiled. "It's a stew, usually made with beef or pork. Well, my grandmother used to make a vegetarian version with potatoes, but traditionally, it's meat and spices. And, I should point out, Hungarians also have a dish they call goulash, but it's more of a soup. The Czech version is heavier."

"Good to know."

"I haven't had it since I moved here." Ondrej looked off into the distance. "Ah, I feel homesick. How about that? I didn't think anything would make me miss Prague, but apparently food will. There are so many good restaurants there now, if nothing else. I could always find something good to eat."

"Maybe you can take me there one day."

"Maybe. After my mother calms down."

Archie thought back to that moment in the den after Ondrej had called home. "Did she not know you're gay? Before you told her about marrying me, I mean."

"She did. She chose to ignore that fact. Now that I'm married, she can't ignore it anymore. Well, she can as long as I'm here and she's in Prague, but not if I introduce you to her." Ondrej let out a sigh. "I'm dreading that, if I'm honest."

"I can see why."

"She's not all bad. Just not the most open-minded person you've ever met."

"Well, there's no rush. But maybe next year, when I can finagle time off, we can travel somewhere."

"Let's wait for my green card to come through. They're stalling it, remember? I don't want to do anything that would jeopardize it."

"The marriage isn't a lie anymore, is it?"

Again, Archie braced himself for Ondrej's answer. Why he kept stumbling this way, why he still doubted Ondrej, he couldn't say, but their relationship still felt unstable.

But Ondrej smiled. "It's not a lie."

Chapter Twenty-One

ARCHIE felt refreshed after the weekend, and he headed into the office Monday morning with resolve and optimism. Maybe his company would go belly-up, but he was determined to do everything in his power to stop that, if only so that he and Ondrej could build a good life together. He didn't like that the future was so unsure, but that morning he didn't have the ill, panicky feeling that had been plaguing him for months.

Marketa stood as he walked by her desk. She followed him into his office.

"Good morning," he said, a little bit alarmed. "What—"

"The mayor's office called. You better call back right away."

"The mayor's office? What on earth—"

"The caller was a Mr. Leonard. He didn't specify what his purpose for calling was, but I gather it was regarding the Eagles stadium project."

The panicky feeling suddenly came back with a vengeance. He sat in his chair, his stomach burbling.

"All right. Give me the number."

When he dialed, he held his breath as he waited for the call to connect. Richard Leonard was the chair of the Department of Buildings, and so much as a thumbs-down from him could torpedo the whole project. After the call went through and Archie introduced himself, Leonard said, "Glad to hear from you, Mr. Katsaros. I understand your firm is interested in developing a new Eagles stadium in Brooklyn."

"Yes, sir."

"I want to tell you, essentially, that the mayor supports the project and wants to be the mayor who presided over the building of a much-beloved new stadium. Because, let's face it, the current Eagles stadium is a shambles."

"Right." Archie wasn't even much of a baseball fan—he could count the number of times he'd been to the current Eagles stadium on one hand—but stories about how beat-up the stadium was had been circulating for years. When the idea for a new stadium had first been pitched to Archie, it was with the understanding that the disrepair at the old stadium was so bad it wasn't worth it to fix it; better to scrap it and start over.

"I support the project too. I'm willing to go to bat for you, Archie. The city doesn't have much money to put toward the project, but we've been approached by a number of corporate backers, and there's the matter of selling the naming rights to the stadium. If you can find a way to finance this thing without creating a boondoggle, you have the full support of the city."

That was good news. Archie had been hoping for some city money, but he'd thought a substantial sum was too much to hope for. "Yes. I have an architect in mind, and of course naming rights was something I'd considered. As for corporate backing, I assumed that—"

Leonard interrupted to rattle off the names of the companies who were interested, mostly banks, plus a major cell phone carrier and a beer brewery in Long Island. Archie found the prospect of negotiating these deals daunting because there was so much ethical murkiness involved. Would accepting money from the beer brewery lock them into only selling their overpriced beer in the stadium? Was that Archie's problem or the Eagles organization's? And if too many corporate players got involved, would acceding to their demands cause the project to go over budget? Because this project could not go over budget without bankrupting Archie.

But the big names involved were also a cause for relief, because if he put together enough corporate backers, this thing might just work out.

"That sounds great," Archie said. "I'd be happy to work with anyone the city approved."

"I'd like you to come in for a meeting with some of the representatives from a few of these companies. I can schedule it for Thursday morning. Would that work?"

"Sounds great."

They banged out the particulars, and as they talked, it was like someone was building supports under Archie. He wanted to do this project so much he could taste it, and hearing that he had backers made it feel more like a reality and less like a pipe dream.

When Archie got off the phone, the first person he called was Ondrej, whom he'd left lounging in bed that morning. He must have caught Ondrej still there, because he answered sleepily.

"We have the backing of the mayor's office," Archie blurted.

"What?"

"For the stadium project. I have a meeting with city officials and the representatives from a number of potential corporate backers on Thursday. I'm willing to put in the work to deal with logistics if I don't have to invest as much of my own money as we originally planned."

"Slow down, Archie. I just woke up. Tell me what happened."

So Archie related what Mr. Leonard had told him and listed the potential backers. It was clear Ondrej had only heard of about half the companies Archie named, and that Ondrej hadn't worked naming rights into the financing equation, but Ondrej said, "Well, if even half of that works out the way you want it to, you might just get the project off the ground after all."

"There are still a lot of things to consider." Archie listed all of his concerns, everything from whether he really wanted one of the banks implicated in mortgage fraud to throw its money at this project or if its name would tarnish Archie's reputation, to the food and beverage companies that wanted to sponsor the project in exchange for giant lit ads over the JumboTron, to which bank or cell phone company they should offer naming rights.

Ondrej listened quietly, occasionally murmuring in response to something Archie said. When Archie asked his opinion, Ondrej just said, "You're finally really thinking like a smart businessman."

"What?" The statement took Archie off guard.

"I know you want to do this project. I know you've been wanting to do it for a while. You get giddy when you talk about it, so much so that your body practically hums. It was making you irrational. But now you're thinking smart, taking everything into consideration." Ondrej paused and then added, "I think you'll be just fine at this meeting, for what it's worth."

"Yeah?"

"Yes. You're asking the right questions."

It meant a lot to Archie that Ondrej thought so. "I'd bring you with me to the meeting if I didn't think it would look strange."

Ondrej laughed. "What, bringing your husband to a business meeting?"

"You're all but a partner in this, you know."

"It's really your company, Archie."

"I know, but you've invested a good deal of money and time into this already."

Archie wished he could see Ondrej's face. He imagined Ondrej was lounging in the big bed—their bed now—naked and stretched out to take up as much space as possible. It was a good image, one that made heat spread through Archie's body.

Ondrej said, "I like the idea of being your partner. I don't know how much I want to be involved directly in the company, but I'm glad that you share what is happening there with me. How long ago was this call with Mr. Leonard?"

"About thirty seconds before I called you."

Ondrej laughed again and it rang through the phone. "You're incredible, you know that? Are you going to take this to the Katsaros board?"

"After the meeting at city hall. I want to have something more concrete to show them before I do."

"Good plan. I tell you what. I won't go with you to the meeting, but I'm around if you want to run anything by me."

"I might take you up on that. Especially Wednesday night when I'm panicking that everyone will think I'm an idiot and withdraw their support for the project."

"They won't."

Ondrej spoke with such certainty that Archie could practically hear the period at the end of that sentence. "It's nice that you think so, but...."

"You're less awkward than you think you are. You can be quite charming when you try. I think there might be something of your father in you after all."

Archie doubted that was true, but he also knew that Ondrej knew it was exactly the sort of compliment he needed. "Thank you."

"I suppose I should get out of this bed, eh?"

"You don't have to. I suppose I could slip out of here at lunchtime to keep you company."

"I'd like that."

As the conversation wound down, Archie found that he was so happy talking to Ondrej that he wanted to blurt out what he'd been feeling in the depths of his soul as he'd dialed the house number to make this phone call: he was utterly, completely, head-over-heels in love with Ondrej.

But perhaps the phone was not the best medium to express that.

"I should get back to work," Archie said, "but I'll try to come home at lunchtime."

"You don't have to if you're busy. I'll see you tonight. I think I'll manage without you until then."

"All right, then. Well, until later."

"Yeah. Well, Archie, I… no, never mind. I'll see you later."

Archie smiled as he hung up the phone.

ONDREJ was still lounging in bed with his laptop propped up on a pillow, half reading the news and half playing mindless puzzle games, when Archie strode into the room.

"You came home at lunch after all," Ondrej said, sitting up.

"You're doing the kept man thing quite well," Archie said. "Maybe I should move the video game console upstairs so you don't even have to leave."

Ondrej grinned. "I'll leave this room eventually. I still have to eat." He closed his laptop and patted the bed next to him. "I honestly wasn't expecting you."

"I've been thinking about you all morning."

Ondrej found that startling. He'd just spent all weekend with Archie—most of it in bed, sure, but they'd spent a lot of time just talking, too—and it seemed impossible that they couldn't spend a few hours apart without yearning for each other. And yet….

Archie sat on the bed. He picked up Ondrej's laptop and placed it on the nightstand. "I wanted to tell you something."

"All right." Ondrej was conscious suddenly of the fact that he was naked under the sheets, but Archie was wearing a suit. It was… kind of sexy, actually. He adjusted the sheets in his lap, because Archie seemed serious and nudity seemed inappropriate.

"I suppose I could have told you over the phone, but there's something so cheap and impersonal about that." He took Ondrej's hand and threaded their fingers together.

"What is it?" Ondrej started wondering about possibilities. The progress with the stadium deal and Archie fretting about the meeting at city hall had probably dominated his morning. Ondrej still had some misgivings about the project, but even he had to admit that an infusion of cash from a number of high-profile corporate sponsors was a step in the right direction.

But something told Ondrej that the stadium was currently far from Archie's mind.

Archie held Ondrej's hand in both of his and gazed at Ondrej affectionately. "I was kidding earlier. I don't actually think you're lazy."

"No, I know." Ondrej put his hand on top of Archie's.

"I think you're so smart, and I know you could do anything you set your mind to, and I appreciate all your help with the company. I couldn't have gotten through any of the last couple of months without you."

"You could have."

"And that's another thing. I know you didn't have much faith in me when you met me, but you do now, and that means the world to me."

"Archie…."

"Let me just say this. I… I love you, Ondrej. It's crazy, I know. I mean, I lusted after you from the first, but now that we've truly gotten to know each other, I feel it deeply. I love you." He laughed, and the sound was so full of joy, it took Ondrej's breath away. "I've been wanting to say it since we got off the phone, so I had to come home to tell you in person, because I... I wanted you to know how happy you make me."

Ondrej's heart pounded. He looked up at Archie and met his gaze. "I feel the same way," he said. "I love you too."

Before Ondrej even had all the words out, Archie surged forward and kissed him. It was fast and hard, a brief but intense meeting of their mouths before Archie backed away again and said, "God, I wish I could stay and make love to you, but I do have to get back."

Ondrej ached with wanting Archie, but he understood that work called. "You really came home just to tell me you love me?"

"Yes. I had to."

Ondrej found he understood that. "I know, I...." And then Ondrej laughed too. "I mean, what the hell is wrong with us? We created a fraud when we got married, and then we had to go and legitimize it by falling in love."

"Crazy." Archie kissed Ondrej again.

Chapter Twenty-Two

THAT first meeting at city hall led to a series of meetings over the next few weeks with a number of potential backers of the stadium project. Each time a meeting went well, Archie felt more confident, which led to him doing well in the meeting after that. It was such a dream as it all fell into place that Archie could hardly believe it.

He was at a meeting with a representative of a bank the first time his personal life was invoked. For weeks, all talk at meetings had been limited to the business at hand or else small talk about the weather. But when Archie met with a rep named Steve Sharp from one of the biggest banks in the country, Ondrej finally came up as a topic of conversation.

"I believe we've met before," Sharp said. "My wife and I attended one of those dreadful fundraisers Marnie

Knox throws. This would have been a few years ago. I'm afraid I can't even remember what she was raising funds for."

"When my father was still alive?" A lot of those events blended together.

"Or it might have been a Met Gala, maybe. But yes, when your father was still alive."

Archie had only been to one Met Gala three years before, when he'd been covertly dating a fashion designer who worked for Michael Kors. "Could be," Archie said. He felt like he had to tread carefully. He never volunteered much about himself in these meetings, especially not with the big corporate bankers, because the financial world tended to be more conservative, in his experience.

"Alexander Katsaros was a delight, as I recall. Wonderful man. I remember him being quite suave. I'm terribly sorry for your loss."

Archie's eyes were itchy suddenly, and he blinked to stave off the surprise burst of emotion he felt. He missed his father most at times like these, when he would have benefitted from the elder Katsaros's advice. "Thank you."

"There's a dinner at the Metropolitan Club this Friday if you're interested in that sort of thing," Sharp said as they wound down the meeting. "It might be a good opportunity to schmooze with a few other potential investors. Davis Morgan will definitely be there, and he's always looking for projects like this."

Davis Morgan was heir to a tremendous fortune, some of the oldest of old New York money; he and Archie had gone to school together, so Archie knew full well who he was. Getting some Morgan money into the project would come with strings but could also help Archie convince others to invest. "Is it a small dinner?" Archie asked.

Sharp shrugged. He was a part of Archie's social world in a way Archie hadn't anticipated, so he knew these dinners could have eight people or they could have five hundred. If it was at the Metropolitan Club, it could have as many as fifty in attendance. "I'm not sure, exactly. But I'm a member at the club, so I could get you an invitation."

"You would do that?"

"I like you, Archie. You surprised me, in a pleasant way. I expected a stuffy prep school kid or someone slick like your father. Not that he was inauthentic, as such. I mean, I knew him a little, but not very well, but he always struck me as the sort of man who could charm you right out of your socks."

"He was."

"But I'm just saying, you seem very down-to-earth, and I think your plans for the project are viable. I'd recommend cutting a few of these costs, but if this project goes as well as I think it will, we'd be happy to have our names on it. Literally, in this case."

"Thank you, sir." It took a lot for Archie not to jump with glee, but he managed to keep his composure because he knew what was expected of him here.

"Forget about the 'sir.' We're friends now. So, dinner Friday. Bring your wife."

Archie took a deep breath. "My husband, actually."

Steve Sharp didn't even blink. "Yes, your husband. I'll have an invitation sent to your office."

ONDREJ dressed carefully, not wanting to match Archie but not wanting to look radically different, either.

"How do I look?" Archie asked, posing in a gray suit with a light pink shirt.

"Very handsome," Ondrej said. He stepped closer to Ondrej and smoothed down his lapels, running his hands over Archie's chest perhaps more than he needed to. "I don't love that your tie matches your shirt, but I suppose that's the trend."

"I like your tie," Archie said, reaching over to finger the violet tie Ondrej was wearing.

"Do I look too much like a banker?"

Archie laughed and leaned over to kiss Ondrej's cheek. "No. Quite the contrary. Everyone else at this party likely will, though."

"Tell me our mission again?"

"We're going to work together to charm Davis Morgan into investing in the stadium."

"And you're old school chums?"

"We went to the same school, yes. I wouldn't say we were chums. I'm hoping he remembers me, but that might be too optimistic."

"All right."

It wasn't like the big charity gala or the yacht party. There was no grand entrance down the staircase or cruise in a luxury boat. This felt nearly mundane by contrast. They left the house together holding hands, and Archie hailed a yellow cab instead of arranging a car service. They arrived at the Metropolitan Club with little fanfare and were ushered into a huge dining room in which there were maybe forty people milling about. It was a more intimate crowd, but Ondrej could smell their money. The women dripped with diamonds and expensive fabric gowns; the men were all in well-tailored suits in very conservative styles. Ondrej fingered his purple tie self-consciously.

"Archie Katsaros!" said a blond man. "So glad you could make it."

"Thank you for inviting me. Inviting us." Archie gestured to Ondrej. "This is my husband, Ondrej."

It felt natural to hear that. Ondrej was Archie's husband in every way now, it seemed. He held out his hand and met Steve Sharp, the banker Archie had met with a few days before.

Ondrej knew this crowd, despite it being full of strangers. He'd been to parties like this with his grandmother. He knew how to behave, how to act like he was thrilled to meet all the terribly boring people, how to eat politely. He hooked his arm around Archie's and made nice with the One Percent of New York.

Steve Sharp went so far as to arrange for Archie and Davis Morgan to be seated beside each other at dinner. Ondrej sat on Archie's other side and tried to overhear the conversation, though the woman sitting beside him, some hedge fund manager's wife, kept trying to engage him in small talk, mostly about fashion, as if the mere fact that Ondrej was gay made him an expert.

Archie was saying, "We did have that class together junior year. American literature, I think."

"Of course, of course. I remember now. Did you have longer hair in high school?"

"I did, yeah. That was my one bit of rebellion, growing my hair long." Archie rubbed his more professional coif.

Davis Morgan chuckled. "Some kids get piercings or tattoos or smoke pot. You grew your hair."

"My father really hated it."

"Oh, but that class. Mrs. Pfeiffer, right?"

They went off on some tangent about teachers they hated in school. The ease of their conversation seemed like a good sign. Discussing their common history as the sons of New York elite who went to some tony school together was a good way to endear Davis Morgan to the cause.

"I bought this off the rack," the woman sitting next to Ondrej said. "But this color was hot on the spring runways. It's not really salmon, right? Kind of a deeper pink."

"Uh-huh," said Ondrej.

"I heard Katsaros is the operation behind the Eagles stadium project," said Morgan, and Ondrej leaned closer to Archie to listen.

Archie grabbed his hand under the table. "Yes. Tentatively, it looks like Pinnacle Bank will be purchasing the naming rights, assuming my board approves it and the deal goes through."

"Ah, yes. Steve mentioned. He does like to put his company's name all over things. Tell me about the plans you have so far."

It was as if Morgan had opened the door just for Archie.

Archie had practiced this very speech with Ondrej many times. He had the stadium elevator pitch down to a science. He could rattle off the information concisely, explaining seating capacity, acreage, affordable housing, and the plan to turn the land the old stadium currently occupied into a park with a huge recreation center to help neighborhood kids.

Morgan nodded along. "I like it. I'll admit, I put a little money into the Barclays Center. I was worried for a while that I'd never see it back, but the return on my investment has defied expectation so far. I've been hoping a similar project would come along. I can't make any promises under the influence of this

fine wine, but I'd like to meet with you to discuss this
further if you're amenable."

"Absolutely," said Archie, not betraying any of
the glee he must have felt at having accomplished his
mission.

Ondrej squeezed his hand.

After the meal, everyone moved to a reception
with after-dinner cocktails in another part of the club,
so Ondrej and Archie split up and mingled with those
assembled. Ondrej wasn't much interested in small talk
with this crowd, but he knew how to play the game well
enough, so he took on the role of the wide-eyed foreign
spouse who was still a little confused about how things
worked in America, and everyone he spoke with ate it
up with a spoon.

He was relieved when the crowd started thinning
and Archie declared he was close to being ready to
leave.

A little while later, as they slipped into the back
of a cab, Archie said, "I'm amazed that went so well."

"I'm glad this is happening for you," Ondrej said.

"For us," Archie said. "I'm doing this for us, you
know. I want to do this project, don't get me wrong, and
I've wanted it since before I met you. But making sure
we have a future, that I don't go bankrupt—that's more
important to me now. I want our relationship to have
a solid foundation, both emotionally and financially."

Ondrej leaned over and kissed Archie's cheek.

The cab let them out in front of the house. Archie
took the first two steps up to the stoop and then turned
around and looked at Ondrej. "I just had a crazy idea."

Ondrej laughed. "What?"

"We've been married, what, almost three months?"

"Yes."

"What if, on our first anniversary, we gave the USCIS a big fuck-you and had a vow renewal ceremony."

"What are you talking about?" Ondrej's heart rate kicked up.

Archie jogged back down the steps and took both of Ondrej's hands in his own. He met Ondrej's gaze, and his eyes sparkled in the yellow haze from the streetlights. "We barely had a wedding, and we had no reception. I don't know how they do things in the Czech Republic, but here, especially for people with money, we have stupid, huge, ostentatious weddings. So let's do that. Have a big, crazy wedding reception to show everyone we're in love for real."

Ondrej laughed and shook his head. "It's a waste of money, Archie. I don't need a big wedding."

"I know. I don't either. I love you, and I believe you when you say you love me. I just thought… okay, nothing ostentatious. But maybe we should throw a party. Have a little ceremony. It's months away, so we have time to plan, I just…." He sighed and looked up at the stars. "We did this backward. At our real wedding, we barely knew each other, but now we do. I want to do it over, and I want to do it right this time. What do you say?"

"You want to renew our vows? And have a fancy reception?" It wasn't that he didn't want to have a big party to celebrate their marriage—Ondrej kind of did, actually—but given their current financial situation, it seemed like such a terrible idea. But the practical and the emotional warred for a moment as Ondrej puzzled out what he wanted if money were no object.

"It doesn't have to be fancy," said Archie. "It should be a celebration, yes, but obviously we won't break the bank throwing it. We could have it at the house, keep the guest list to only our real friends and not half of New York."

"So a modest celebration?"

"Whatever you want, Ondrej." Archie squeezed Ondrej's hands.

"Are you… are you proposing to me?"

Archie smiled, and it was incandescent. "I suppose that I am. Ondrej Kovac? Will you remarry me?"

Ondrej laughed. "Of course, Archie."

Archie hugged him and gave him a quick kiss on the lips. "I love you, Ondrej. So much."

"I love you too."

Epilogue

AMY fiddled with Ondrej's tie as they stood in his former bedroom in the house he shared with Archie. The room had reverted back into a guest room, though Ondrej still kept his off-season clothes in the closet. It was currently an ideal place to lie low before having to be seen by the crowd gathering downstairs.

"Did you see Priscilla Zimmer's article about this?" Ondrej asked. "She's decided that this vow-renewal ceremony is all for show, and the fact that we're having it at all is a sign our marriage is on the rocks."

Amy stepped back and admired her handiwork. "That's nonsense, you know."

"*I* know that. I wonder if New York society is thinking the same thing, though. They probably are. Nobody believes people's intentions are true."

"Who cares? You love Archie. You're renewing your vows because you were too busy to have a proper wedding when you got married. It's not like public opinion will break you up."

"True."

"At least they're over thinking this is a green card marriage. I haven't seen Zimmer mention that in weeks."

"You read society tabloids?"

Amy shrugged and fiddled with Ondrej's lapels. "I suppose you look acceptable."

Ondrej laughed. "Thank you."

"You know you're a very handsome man and Archie is lucky to have you."

Ondrej grinned at that.

They'd cleared some of the junk out of the formal living room and put it in storage so that they could use the room for this purpose. The plan was for Archie and Ondrej to renew their vows in front of the hearth as everyone sat in comfortable chairs and looked on, before moving to dinner in the formal dining room. Archie seemed glad to be using the rooms of his house for their intended purpose instead of letting the furniture fester.

Amy led Ondrej into the formal living room, where Archie already waited, resplendent in a soft-gray suit. Archie smiled.

The room wasn't very crowded, limited only to Archie and Ondrej's real friends. The officiant leading the ceremony was the elderly minister of the church Archie had grown up in. A few of Archie's extended family members, including Sam and Todd and Archie's goddaughter, were in the assembled crowd. Ondrej wished he could have said the same, but his mother had flatly declined the invitation. His father had sent a present and a nice card, so they were making progress, but they hadn't quite come around yet. Maybe they would, but Ondrej didn't want to count on it. It seemed to gall Archie that Ondrej's family wasn't coming, but Ondrej hadn't been very surprised.

So they said their vows, this time staring into each other's eyes and holding hands. It was so utterly different from the sterile completion of paperwork at city hall when they'd gotten married. Now Ondrej promised to give his whole heart to Archie, to be with him through good times and bad, to love him as they grew old together. Archie had a faint smile on his face and a tear in his eye as he repeated the same vow. When they kissed, everyone clapped.

"I do love you," Archie said, hugging Ondrej tight. "More today than yesterday."

"I love you too. I'm glad you talked me into this."

Over dinner a little while later, Archie clinked his glass with a knife and stood.

"You're doing it backwards!" Amy said. "You're supposed to kiss when *we* clink *our* glasses."

"I will happily kiss my husband all day long," Archie said, "but before I do that, I want to announce something."

Everyone went quiet.

"I wasn't going to do this here," Archie said, "but I'm so excited I don't want to wait. So you're hearing it here first. The city gave the Eagles stadium project the green light yesterday."

The crowd offered some applause. It had been slow going—arranging the funding, getting the proposal right, hiring the right people. All the while, Archie had followed through on his and Ondrej's plans to make the company more efficient. For the first time in two years, they had turned a profit in the most recent quarter, and Archie was delighted about that too. It was a modest profit, but they were in the black just the same, and it seemed like things were headed in the right direction. He'd even persuaded Dan Preston to back down from his calls to sell off major parts of the company.

"Anyway, I also wanted to welcome you all and thank you for coming. Some of you know the path Ondrej and I took to get here was not exactly the usual way of things, but I could not be happier now that we're both here." He turned and looked at Ondrej with so much love and affection in his eyes, it stole Ondrej's breath.

So Ondrej stood too. "I'm happy too," he said.

Archie took Ondrej's hand and picked up his glass of champagne. "Let's have a toast. To a wonderful future together!"

"To the future!" the crowd echoed.

Ondrej clinked his glass against Archie's, but instead of sipping the champagne, he gave Archie a kiss. Because, unlike a year ago, the world seemed full of possibilities, especially with Archie at his side.

Later, after the caterers had cleared the formal living room and people were dancing to music Amy had chosen for the occasion—kicky pop music instead of old, slow jazz—Ondrej hung on Archie as they danced together. He held Archie close, rested his chin on Archie's shoulder, and breathed in his scent.

When the music slowed down, he said, "When you stood up at dinner, I was worried for a moment you'd tell everyone our *other* news."

Archie sighed happily. "No, not yet. I'm thrilled about the stadium getting the go-ahead, but I'm even more excited about the other thing, and I don't want to jinx it."

Ondrej thought it was strange to refer to the child they were set to adopt as "the other thing," but he understood Archie's discretion when Cathleen Brandt interrupted them to insist they take a photo together. It was impossible to speak privately at an event at which they were the center of attention. But Ondrej did share Archie's sentiment that the child—they knew only it was a boy and he was due to be born in three months—was far more exciting. Their contact at the adoption agency had told them not to count on this quite yet because birth mothers changed their minds all the time, but Ondrej felt in his gut that it would happen. He felt like his whole life was falling into place.

After they posed for photos, Archie swept Ondrej back into his arms.

Ondrej said, "When I moved to New York, I wanted adventure."

"I know."

"This wasn't what I imagined, but I'm excited to have these adventures with you."

Archie smiled. "Me too."

Coming in August 2016

#15

Stranded with Desire by Vivien Dean and Rick R. Reed

CEO Maine Braxton and his invaluable assistant, Colby, don't realize they share a deep secret: they're in love—with each other. That secret may have never come to light but for a terrifying plane crash in the Cascade Mountains that changes everything.

In a struggle for survival, the two men brave bears, storms, and a life-threatening flood to make it out of the wilderness alive. The proximity to death makes them realize the importance of love over propriety. Confessions emerge. Passions ignite. They escape the wilds renewed and openly in love.

When they return to civilization, though, forces are already plotting to snuff out their short-lived romance and ruin everything both have worked so hard to achieve.

#16

Marriage of Inconvenience by M.J. O'Shea

Kerry Pickering has a problem. As a publicist for Hollywood bad boy Jericho Knox, it's Kerry's job to keep Jericho in the news. So far, Jericho's partying and public escapades have made it easy. But Jericho has a secret, and when that secret is revealed in the most spectacularly disastrous way, it's up to Kerry to spin it.

The team decides the best course of action is to make the public fall in love—with Jericho's secret committed relationship. The one that doesn't exist. Yet.

The team wants someone they can trust. Someone in the inner circle. That someone is Kerry. But what will happen when Kerry realizes that for him, the romance is no longer pretend? Can Jericho love him back, or is he just playing a role?

www.dreamspinnerpress.com

Now Available

ⓓREAMSPUN DESIRES

#11

Finding Family by Connie Bailey

When you find your family, you'll do anything to keep it.

When Charles Macquarrie inherits a fortune and an international clothing company, he also inherits three young cousins he desperately needs help raising. By a stroke of luck, he discovers and hires Jonathan Lamb, who spent his life in a children's home due to chronic illness, to be his nanny.

If Jon thought a budding romance with his wealthy boss complicated his life, he has no idea of the hardships awaiting him when he's charged with embezzlement. But even when threatened by accounting discrepancies and mob connections, Jon and Charles won't let go of the family they've built together without a fight.

#12

Undercover Boyfriend by Jacob Z. Flores

Two men, one lie, and a whole bunch of trouble.

Marty Valdez is in serious trouble. His sister's wedding is around the corner, and everyone expects to meet Marty's super-successful underwear model boyfriend—who Marty invented. Now Marty has to produce a half-naked hottie or suffer the worst humiliation of his life.

FBI agent Luke Myers is in serious trouble. He's been working undercover to take down a dangerous drug cartel, but his cover's blown and he needs to disappear. Luckily, a geeky yet intriguing comic book artist gives him the perfect opportunity. Luke just has to pretend to be his boyfriend, and pretending is what he does best. But between Marty's mother and his ex, Luke might've bitten off more than he can chew, and Marty's knack for finding trouble might ruin more than just his sister's wedding.

www.dreamspinnerpress.com

Love Always Finds a Way

AUG 0 3 2019

CPSIA information can be obtained
at www.ICGtesting.com
Printed in the USA
FFHW021704190719
53734378-59429FF